## *"You're meeting someone. Who is it?"*

His head swiveled violently from side to side. "I don't know."

Before the man could even blink, I lifted the knife and let it fall a second time, entering the palm effortlessly. "Someone is trying to kill me, my friend. I get impatient when I'm hunted. So far I've been gentle, but next time . . ."

The understanding he showed was that of a shattered man. "What do you wish to know?"

"Who hired you? . . ."

# NICK CARTER IS IT!

"Nick Carter out-Bonds James Bond."
—*Buffalo Evening News*

"Nick Carter is America's #1 espionage agent."
—*Variety*

"Nick Carter is razor-sharp suspense."
—*King Features*

"Nick Carter is extraordinarily big."
—*Bestsellers*

"Nick Carter has attracted an army of addicted readers . . . the books are fast, have plenty of action and just the right degree of sex . . . Nick Carter is the American James Bond, suave, sophisticated, a killer with both the ladies and the enemy."
—*The New York Times*

# FROM THE NICK CARTER
## KILLMASTER SERIES

# A Killmaster Spy Chiller

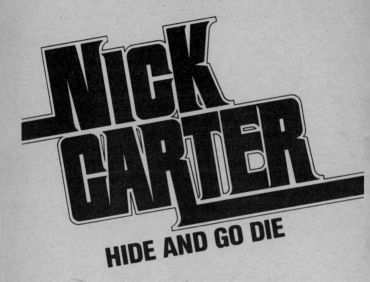

## NICK CARTER

### HIDE AND GO DIE

CHARTER BOOKS, NEW YORK

HIDE AND GO DIE

A Charter Book/published by arrangement with
The Condé Nast Publications, Inc.

PRINTING HISTORY
Charter edition/April 1983

ISBN: 0-441-33068-1

Charter Books are published by Charter Communications, Inc.
200 Madison Avenue, New York, N.Y. 10016.
PRINTED IN THE UNITED STATES OF AMERICA

*Dedicated to the men of the
Secret Services of the
United States of America*

# ONE

I, Nick Carter, felt good as I entered the tower of steel wherein resided my opulent tower suite.

Good?

Hell, I felt terrific, filled with anticipation. I was between assignments, and it looked like I would stay that way for a while. And cradled on my arm was one of the most delectable women I'd ever had the pleasure of chasing but not quite capturing.

I had high hopes that the chase would come to an end within the hour.

I hadn't been quite as high earlier that afternoon. I was just one among many D.C. commuters, one solitary soul among the multitude moving in fitful stops and starts in jammed-up traffic. I had been drifting with infuriated helplessness, one hand resting lightly on the wheel, the other on the car's open window propping my chin.

Wearily I had been casting bemused glances at the endless carnival of rubble, glass, and steel, feeling my impatience mounting, when I suddenly saw my solution to the infernal congestion and exhaust fumes.

Before the traffic broke free onto the freeway and across the bridge, the signs beckoned in endless, insistent redundancy: MOTEL BAR MOTEL BAR MOTEL BAR. The neon cherries in the neon martini glasses glowed like coals from hell. Livid green tropical leaves and cartooned palm trees and hula girls wriggled and winked and spelled out DRINK, RELAX, DANCE, FUN, COCKTAILS, GIRLS, FOAM MATTRESSES, HEATED SWIMMING POOL.

Just what I needed: a drink.

Five minutes later I was sipping a cool one.

Fifteen minutes later I was chatting with an old friend.

"Rebecca, really . . . you're divorced now? How about dinner?"

Dinner was wonderful.

And now we were heading to my apartment.

I firmly believed *that* would be wonderful as well.

"Evening, Mr. C."

I gave a pleasant nod to the portly doorman, whose name I could never quite remember, and guided my lady into the elevator.

"Ten?" she said, lifting an eyebrow as I pushed the button.

"Ten, the top," I replied with a smile, and leaned back to let my eyes take her all in.

She had a svelte lushness to her body, with full breasts and a well-rounded rear end. That, added to the appeal of a lovely face and a head of hair like spun gold, made for one knockout woman.

"Are you still with the old firm, Nick?"

"Sure . . . play and pray for retirement."

Her sensual lips curved into a nice smile.

Of course, she knew "the old firm" as Amalgamated Press and Wire Services. Which it was.

Amalgamated is located in Washington's Dupont Circle, and to the world, it is the number three news pusher.

But to those who know its real purpose, it is the cover designation for AXE, a top secret, highly sensitive branch of U.S. intelligence. David Hawk is its founder and head taskmaster.

My designation: N3, Killmaster.

I do not usually desert for parts unknown without giving the Old Man some indication of my whereabouts. But the last mission had taken its toll on me. It had been a rather grisly affair, involving an assassination attempt in the Middle East. My main problem was that the attempt had succeeded.

I do not deal well with failure.

With the aid of two other killmasters, N7 and N12, we had managed to keep the carnage limited to the political leader himself, but the effort had cost my fellow agents their lives.

Death is no stranger in my business. He is a constant . . . like a pulse. But his stench gets heavier the closer to home he gets.

N7 and N12 were just too close to home.

So I craved retreat, a brief respite to clear my nostrils and clear my brain. I had gone seeking simplicity in the hills of Virginia, and I had found it. I had also very quickly gotten bored. Too much fresh air and green grass.

Hence my return to Washington that afternoon, and . . . Rebecca.

Again I sliced my eyes across that lush figure, and rocked forward and back on my heels. With any luck I would not be bored this evening.

"Ya know, Nick, it's always been hard for me to think of you as a correspondent."

"Oh, really? Why is that?"

She laughed. It was a fine, light sound, like a clear bell.

"Oh, I don't know. You always seemed the sinister, rugged type . . . like a spy or something, ya know?"

"*Me?* Nah . . . I'd be scared to death."

As the elevator door slid open, I picked up my bag and allowed her to precede me into the hall. I followed, chuckling slightly as she scanned the hall uncertainly. She studied each of the hallway's six doors, waiting for me to lead her to the correct one.

I paused and gestured expansively. "Ten-A, m'lady. Your brandy awaits."

She smiled warmly, displaying none of the tentativeness I feared might come from knowing me "pre-divorce," and led us off toward what I hoped would be heaven. I watched admiringly as her buttocks did battle with the smooth polyester of her slacks.

She halted at the door while I fumbled in my pocket for the keys.

"Don't you just love that mural?" I said, nodding my head to the wall across from the entrance.

On the end of my key chain is a tiny infrared flashlight designed to look like a medallion: an ingenious bauble courtesy of AXE R and D. I pressed it as she looked away, concentrating the beam around the doorframe. The field strips were in place, just as I had left them.

I released the "medallion" and placed the key into the first lock as she turned back to the doorway. "It's nice," she purred. "Why so many locks? It doesn't seem to be a bad neighborhood."

"Just cautious," I answered. What I did not tell her was that the four locks were the necessary part of a dangerous vocation. Each of the four must be opened in sequence—and with specific timing—or the person stepping in is showered with lethal gas.

She filled the time with chatter. "What are your neighbors like? Anything like you?" The last was said with definite admiration.

"Don't really know them," I answered. "Amalgamated keeps me on the road pretty much and no one ever seems to use the laundry room when I do."

She giggled as I threw open the door and gestured her in. Her eyes flickered around the room as I dumped my bags and sealed us in. As I did so, I gave a quick glance at the thermostat flanking the door.

Inside it are three tiny lights, each meant to communicate something to me. If Hawk had tried to summon me, a blue light would be registered; if any of the AXE staff had availed themselves of the facility, a green light would show. If my apartment had been entered, a red light would display itself.

Only two lights were on. The red one, signifying my own entry, and the blue one, indicating an attempt by Hawk to reach me.

I cursed the blue light. It had been my hope that I might have skipped town without Hawk's knowledge. But the blue in the dial meant the chief was right now pacing his office, undoubtedly cursing my name.

I thought of reporting in, but then reconsidered. Rebecca was waiting, and what difference would one or two hours make in an already irresponsible flight?

"Let me kick on some air," I said as I hit the "fan" switch. Both the blue and red lights blinked out. Had the apartment been entered since Friday, the red light would have remained.

"The apartment is beautiful," Rebecca whispered. "Did you decorate it yourself?"

"Well," I replied, turning to face her, "I did have a little professional help."

"You've got to give me the name," she said, her head turning in a slow circle.

She didn't know it, but I couldn't tell her. The name would never be shared. The apartment—in fact the whole building—was just another of AXE's creations.

AXE believed its agents should live well. It was one of the surest ways of keeping the competition from overbidding.

*A pampered agent is a loyal agent,* was their perceptive philosophy.

"Are the other apartments this nice?"

I grinned at her as I headed toward the bar. "I already told you, I don't really know the other people on the floor. I'm just not around enough."

I wasn't lying, exactly. I didn't know the others on the floor because there were no others. The entire top floor was mine, the floors below peopled by AXE staffers. The doors in the hallway were all bogus, numbers and all—all, that is, but two. One working door was the one through which we had just entered; the other was the door to 10-F, a second means of entry or escape should the need arise. The rest were all facade, backed by sheet steel and as impenetrable as a nun's bedroom.

"Apartment" 10-B was an enormous gym, accessible through a panel in my bedroom wall; 10-C was a small computer and viewing room; 10-D and 10-E were an arsenal and shooting range; and 10-F a dressing room containing a vast wardrobe of disguises.

"I'm impressed as hell," she sighed.

I poured the brandy as she gawked. "You should be," I grinned. "I have it on very good authority that George Washington himself slept here. Of course, I also have it on good authority that George Washington seems to have slept just about everywhere."

She wriggled over to me and picked up her brandy, her lovely round bottom pushing itself onto the barstool as she giggled, "What I wonder, is whether *Mrs.* Washington slept with him!"

I smiled at the wickedness in her eyes and lifted my glass. "To good old Martha. Let's hope that while

George was sleeping here, she was bouncing the bed-springs at his side."

Glasses clinked, and good brandy slipped down thirsty throats.

"You're fun . . . you know that?" she said, her blue eyes twinkling.

"Of course I do. I work at it!"

A second round was poured and downed; this time the toast a silent one to each other. Without discussion, I came out from behind the bar, and she rose to join me. Our lips met, and her lush body pressed hungrily against mine. The kiss was long and deep.

When we finally broke, she tilted her flushed face up to mine, and her voice was low and husky when she spoke. "It's your house. You direct the traffic."

I inclined my head toward the bedroom, and silently we moved toward it. She nuzzled herself into me, placing my free hand over her luscious breast. I stopped at the door, unwilling to release my charge but eager for the events to come. I fondled her a moment, then slowly released my grip to reach for the door's handle. Just as quickly, I froze.

A thin crack of light was peering down the side. The door was not closed, and it was not me who had left it that way. Impatiently, Rebecca slid her hand toward the knob. I grabbed it with a speed and forcefulness that momentarily shocked her.

"Wait!" I roared.

Her eyes opened wide. "Wha . . . I thought . . . ."

"Oh, you thought right, Rebecca. It's just that . . . ."

"What?"

*Come on, Carter, you're an accomplished liar. What the hell did you just think . . . ?*

"Breakfast."

"Huh . . . ?"

"I don't have a damn thing for breakfast."

"Nick, darling." Her arms wound around my neck and her breasts drilled holes in my chest. "You're all the sustenance I need, tonight . . . or tomorrow morning."

"No . . . got to have breakfast later . . . after . . . in the morning. It's the Continental in me!"

She was anything but convinced as I shuttled her away from the door.

"It'll be great," I continued. "There's a deli only a block down the street. You go pick up some food . . . simple stuff, you know—some good bread and cheese. And while you're gone, I'll . . . uh . . . get everything ready."

"Ready?"

"Yeah . . . fold back the covers, light some candles, plump the pillows . . ."

She was still not convinced. So I turned her, pulled her into me, and hit her with a Nick Carter special . . . a kiss guaranteed to reach clear down to her toes. Her body stiffened, then melted. I broke the kiss and hugged her to me, whispering in her ear. "Don't take too long, okay?"

She took one second to catch her breath, then sped for the door. "Be back in a second!" she giggled, and tore open the door.

"Leave it open," I called after her. "Just a crack. I want to be ready for you when you get back, and I don't want to have to appear in the doorway. It would be one hell of a way to meet the neighbors."

Another giggle and she was gone. I moved to the door and waited until I heard the elevator come and go before stepping into the hall. I pulled the key ring from my pocket and moved over to door 10-F. I focused the medallion on the door seam. The field strips were not in place.

I turned the key ring and inserted the key. This door, like the other, had its specific sequence and timing. But unlike the door to my apartment, this sequence was registered at headquarters. It was sometimes necessary for others to use the facilities, and this sequence was therefore registered with AXE Internal Security Division. In the interest of privacy, the locks on my door were a sequence of my own invention, the sliding panel into the gym operable only from my side of the panel.

An icy chill shuddered through my spine as I registered Fact Number One: the intruder knew the sequence.

I opened the door carefully, half expecting to find the intruder's body, and snapped on the light. The room was devoid of all but the racks of outfits and the makeup table.

I focused my attention around the room, bringing into play my photographic recall. Nothing had been moved. I grabbed a nearby chair and elevated myself up to the first sprinkler head dangling from the ceiling. I had to be sure the sequence had been violated by procedure. It was always possible, with several intruders, that one or two had been gassed, and others available to remove the bodies.

I lifted the ceiling tile from above the sprinkler and checked the container that fed into it. None of the gas had been released.

Fact Number Two: The intruder or intruders knew the sequence *and* its system. AXE security had been violated.

I replaced the tile and stepped down from the chair. It was time to consider motive. I had to rule out AXE's use of the facility. Had there been any authorized entry, the field strips would have been replaced and the use logged on the thermostat in my apartment. The only lights I had seen had been the summons from Hawk and my own entry.

That left only outside interference.

Accepting that, I had to determine the "why." Only two motives seemed plausible: theft or assassination. Either someone entered to remove something, or someone entered to leave something. I wouldn't know the answer to the first option until I reached the computer area, the only rooms worth stealing from.

I would have to consider the second option to get there.

I knelt down and scanned the floor. There were no trip cords visible, but that didn't rule out some sort of pressure-sensitive plate stashed beneath the rug. I examined the baseboards. In order to get under the rug, the baseboards would need to be stripped. I examined the top seam carefully, looking for any cracks in the paint where it abutted the wall. There were none.

That left only heat, sound, and electronic or radio waves as detonating mechanisms.

I exited back through the door and walked as silently as I could down to the end of the hall. I flipped open the fuse box and unlocked a tiny cubicle situated at the bottom. Inside were seven circuit breakers and three dials.

I turned the first dial and waited while the heat lamps in each of the floor's rooms kicked into high gear. It would take two minutes to find out if there were any heat-sensitive devices planted in the complex.

There were not. Heat was out.

Next I turned the second dial. I waited while the green light flashed, telling me that recorded conversations were being fed into the floorwide sound system. I moved on to the third dial, turning it one number at a time, filling each room in turn with blaring noise.

Nothing. Rule out sound.

I then moved over to the circuit breakers, hitting each and killing the circuitry into each room. Again, nothing. There were no internal electronic trips. That left only external. I flipped the final switch, setting up the building's radio-interference system. Again, nothing. There were no external signals reaching the floor.

I reset the box, all but the radio scrambler, and sealed it.

I returned to the costume room. I would have to move quickly. Rebecca wouldn't spend forever at the deli, especially after the buildup I had given her. I paused at the entry to the arsenal and range, and checked again for any mechanical or battery-operated triggers.

Zero.

I repeated my scan, again utilizing my photographic memory. Nothing had been tampered with . . . visibly, that is. I couldn't afford to check the drawers; it was always possible they had been rigged. Logic told me that there was nothing worth stealing aside from some classic firearms. If robbery were the motive, the next room would tell the tale.

I moved on to the computer room.

Once more there was no apparent disturbance. To be sure, I stepped to the back of the console and removed the panel. The wiring was intact, with no lethal additions. I stepped back to the front and keyed in a command for regressive retrieval.

Regressive retrieval is a private addition to the computer, one I wired in myself. Since the facilities are sometimes used by AXE staffers, I gain a certain sadistic pleasure in being able to reproduce their work on the computer. All entries, requests and printouts are automatically displayed, starting with the most recent and working back. It's my own secret coding, my own private joke.

The spy spying on the spies.

What it would yield now, however, was any information my intruders may have tried to gain. If theft was the motive, the computer would be their only target. The most recent entry flashed itself onto the screen. It was my own. No one had touched the machine since I had.

Robbery was out.

I shut down the computer and moved on again, working my way into the gym. If someone were going to nail me, this would be the most likely spot. The gym was a regular feature of my daily routine. If any of the various pieces of equipment were rigged, I would no doubt find myself bench-pressing the Pearly Gates.

I went over the room as carefully and quickly as events would allow. Again I came up empty. I was about to surrender to total confusion when something caught my eye. Again, there was a thin ribbon of light where none should have been.

The panel to my bedroom had been found and breached.

A momentary anger rose within me. There is a sense of violation akin to rape when one's own inner sanctum has been entered. To attack the business end of my life is to give me what I expect and deserve. I have done more than my fair share of raping where the enemy is concerned.

But to drag the fight into my own home is unforgivable.

I circled back through the rooms and sealed 10-F behind me. I then reentered my apartment, glad to see that Rebecca was still out, and approached the bedroom door. I grabbed one of the Russian sabers decorating my wall and pressed the tip into the center of the door.

I leaned back against the wall, comfortable with the AXE implanted shielding beneath the sheet rock. It would take nothing short of an atomic blast to penetrate their precautions. In one swift gesture I jammed at the sword, then watched as the door swung open.

Nothing.

I replaced the sword, then searched this room as I had the others, starting beneath the bed. There are too many people around familiar with my tastes and desirous of my death to overlook the obvious. The mattress had not been tampered with, ditto the remainder of the room. That left only the living room.

I stepped back into it and scanned the surroundings. I didn't catch it immediately, but soon I found my eyes drawn to the bar. Something had changed. I focused my recall and soon had the answer. There was an empty bottle of Glenlivet scotch sitting on the bar shelf, a bottle that had been one-quarter full when I left on Friday.

I went over and examined it carefully. Nothing was out of the ordinary. I then knelt down and checked the supply below. A fresh bottle stood staring on the shelf, a thin thread of nylon cording taped to its base. One careless grasp at the bottle and I would have found myself strung out on a hangover from which I would never have recovered.

As I said, they know my tastes.

The question now was how to defuse it. There was no getting at it from behind. Faint fragments of wood and dust told me the explosives were planted in the wall. Without being able to see the bomb itself, I couldn't determine whether the trip was contact or pressure.

The best option seemed to be to await the return of my shapely blond bombshell and whisk her off to the nearest motel while AXE's bomb squad did the dirty work.

But there was still a residue of anger over the rape of my premises. I debated dealing with the device myself.

My decision was made for me. I could hear the elevator doors opening in the hall and the click of Rebecca's clogs as she stepped out. I stood up and turned, preparing the speech that would usher us both out of harm's way. But as I was preparing my case, a high-pitched, sonic squeal suddenly pierced the air behind me.

The bomb was activating on its own.

It was then the whole horrible picture dawned on me.

Whoever had laid the trap had done their homework well. There was no need to rig the apartment with a detonator. The whole floor was mine. One had only to place a trip on the elevator itself, and the likely victim would be yours truly. Although others did use the facilities, it was a rare event. One had only to rig the trip for sequence, and the odds were a hundred-to-one I would be the passenger. Since the apartment had to have been entered since Friday, one trip was all that had to be considered for outsiders.

The elevator comes up once to deposit strangers, and then comes up once more to take them away! The next trip has to be me.

I moved even as the full ramifications were pouring over me. If the first trip *was* me, the detonator bottle would do the trick. If it was not me, the next trip *would* be.

Three trips. One to bring Rebecca and me up, one to take her down to the deli, one to bring her back. The third time's the charm.

Fact Number Three: The assassin was an insider!

The only small consolation I possessed as I hurled myself toward the door was that the bomb would have to be timed to allow me to enter the apartment. There would be the walk down the hall, and the time necessary for the locks. Anything after that was strictly borrowed.

Rebecca was just inching in the door when I hit it. I piled into her, sending groceries sailing into the hallway.

I grabbed at her, refusing to allow her to stumble as I drove my momentum hard to our right. Together, we staggered and then fell, shielded by the rigid security of the AXE-made interior wall.

The explosion, when it came, buckled the wall on the apartment side to its limits, but it held. Pictures lifted from their hooks and crashed to the carpeted floor while vases were jarred from the three hallway tables. The door blew from its hinges and tumbled to the floor, but that was the extent of the damage.

I rolled my head back to study the scene, only vaguely aware of the small scream building in Rebecca's throat. When I turned back to take inventory of her, panic was bleeding its way rapidly to the surface. I struggled for words to calm and confuse her, but the only thing that managed to come out was:

"I guess somebody didn't like one of my stories."

The resultant shock was enough to twist her scream into a distorted giggle. Her shock released, she turned to flight. She leaped for the elevator, her hands slamming at the buttons.

The last thing I saw were those gloriously coordinated buttocks moving hurriedly into the elevator.

And then she was gone.

I turned, lit a tailor-made, gold-tipped cigarette, and surveyed the debris.

What would Hawk say?

"Bloody insufferable."

What did I say?

"Shit."

And it had nothing to do with the debris.

# TWO

There was a horrifying sense of déjà-vu as I stepped into Amalgamated's main floor. It was as though AXE itself had been bombed. Staffers were flying to and fro, while cartloads of records were being moved with frenzied determination. I started off toward Hawk's office only to have my progress checked at frequent intervals by strange new faces, all demanding full security identification and procedure.

By the time I reached the boss's quarters, I was totally confused. I stepped into the outer office, fully expecting the gorgeous vision of Hawk's secretary, Ginger Bateman, but finding instead the rather prunish features of some ancient harridan. She rose to halt me. It was yet another assault on my senses, and in frustration and disgust I waved her off, passing on directly into Hawk's aerie.

It was with a certain relief that I greeted Hawk's frosty gray head bowed over his desk. "What in the hell is going . . ." was as far as I got in my inquiry before the callused edge of a human hand impacted itself against the back of my neck. I hit the floor and rolled, ready to face whatever awaited.

Once my vision had cleared, I was relieved to find the face that greeted me a friendly one.

16

"Goddammit, Carter! You trying to give me a heart attack, or what?"

My hand pressed at the back of my neck. "Right now, I'd be content with something a bit more lingering and painful," I answered.

Qualley reached down and helped me to my feet. "Jesus," he sputtered, "you just barged in here. Haven't you ever heard of following procedure? That witch sitting out there sure as hell ain't there for decoration."

I glared up at the man towering over me. Bill Qualley was a good agent, designation N17. But on a social level, he had all the sophistication of a clip-on bow tie. I turned to address my grievances to Hawk.

"I'm afraid I've got some bad news . . ." But once more, my progress was halted. I stared in amazement at the rigid stillness of the figure behind the desk. It was Hawk right down to the weathered features and the chewed-up cigar in his right hand. But it was not Hawk. Instead, it was a letter-perfect wax reproduction. I circled the desk and stared.

"Scary, ain't it?" Qualley growled.

Its purpose dawned on me with a vengeance. "Jesus," I gasped. "Someone's going to make a try for the Old Man?"

Qualley shrugged. "That's the only thing I can figure. All I know is I got a Code-7 recall, and as soon as I show up here, they hustle my butt up to this office, plop me down without so much as a copy of *Penthouse* to pass the time, and tell me to guard this oversize candle."

My mind jolted.

Code-7 was the highest priority recall in the AXE system. It required all agents to desert the field, mission or not, and hightail it to the Amalgamated complex itself. For a Code-7 to be even contemplated required a crisis of the highest order.

"Actually," Qualley chuckled, "it's not so bad. I've been unloading every complaint I've ever had about this job to that silent mug. Kinda fun, in a way."

I was suddenly in no mood for the wit and wisdom of Bill Qualley. "Do you know where Hawk is?"

Again Qualley shrugged. "He checked in about an hour ago. Said he was headed down to Trainee Observation. You might still find him there."

I thanked him, and then I moved through the outer office, bowing gallantly to Ginger Bateman's indignant replacement, and made for Trainee Observation.

The room itself was down the hall and to the right, a glass-encased viewing section that overlooked the huge training room below. As I entered, I was greeted once more by the mane of silver hair that signified David Hawk. This time the figure was the living, breathing, cigar-smoking original.

As I closed the door quietly behind me, I was struck by the fact that the real Hawk was no more animated than his wax counterpart. The man sat stock-still, his eyes perusing the amassed crop of rookie trainees in the room below, and his mood one of severe contemplation. What was even more jarring was the atmosphere of depression that smothered the room. Hawk was not given to emotions, and if he was feeling them now, something of supreme import had to be motivating him.

He was, as yet, unaware of my intrusion, and I used the respite to frame an explanation of my weekend's disappearance. Then I cleared my throat and launched into my speech. "Sir, I'm sorry I've been incommunicado—"

My excuses were cut off by the sudden leap of Hawk's frame. He whirled to face me, his ashen face an odd blending of joy and amazement, his voice hoarse with emotion. "Nick! You're alive!"

Two thoughts ran simultaneously through my brain,

both significant as well as confusing. The first was that the man was indeed under severe strain. His use of my first name was cause enough to challenge his sanity. Moments of such warmth and intimacy were jewels to be treasured.

But as to his surprise that I was still alive . . . was it possible that Hawk already knew of the attempt on my life? I had come straight to Amalgamated after the blast, and I'd told no one that our "secret" little arrangement at the apartment was no longer secret.

Something was definitely strange here.

My brow furrowed as I stepped down toward him. "It's me, sir. In the flesh, but only by the skin of my teeth."

Hawk's look darkened. "What do you mean?"

I studied him a moment. "You mean, you don't know about the explosion? Then wha—"

"Talk to me, Nick. Tell me exactly what happened."

I explained the bomb attempt, adding that AXE would need to give my apartment a security once-over in case there were secondary charges. His response was silent intake, followed by another uncharacteristic outburst of emotion. But this time, it was raw hatred.

"That bastard! That son-of-a-bitching bastard!"

I raised my palms to stem the tide. "Hold it, sir. There's something going on, and I think it's about time I found out what it was."

Hawk checked his outburst, and with a heavy sigh, he returned to his seat, his eyes traveling once more to the trainees below.

"What do you think, N3?" he asked as I took the seat next to him. I took his return to the use of my formal designation as a return to normalcy. "Think any of them will turn out to be agents?"

I looked at the motley crew below before answering. "The usual percentage will make it, I guess. What do we usually get? One out of a hundred, maybe?"

"Usually," he replied. "But this group is different. They will *all* make it. They've got to. They won't be good, but they'll make it!"

I stared over at the man, baffled by the resignation in his voice. "Care to explain?"

He popped the cigar into his mouth and gave it a reassuring chew before quietly responding. "Two days ago, AXE achieved another first. We've had our first defection."

The words could not have hit me any harder if Hawk had bellowed them. Defection is the greatest fear of any covert organization. That a defecting agent carries with him the knowledge of his organization is bad enough, but when the organization itself is a well-guarded secret, as it is with AXE, the departure is even more frightening.

"Who?" I asked, my own voice taking on the pervading depression of the room.

There was another pause, and an audible swallow, before Hawk answered. The words, when they came, were simple and destructive. "N1."

"Christ," was all I could mutter before the room dropped into silence. There was no need for further comment. Hawk's mood was suddenly mirrored in my own guts.

Theodore Salonikos, designation N1.

Theo had been the very first, and his relationship to Hawk was one of far greater intimacy and depth than that of agent and control. He had been part of the birth of AXE. He had been occupying the seat next to Hawk when the first virgin batch of rookies entered the room below . . . the very group that had contained myself. It was Theo who had handed me my certificate of approval and walked me through the first few missions.

Theo had entered the world in a tiny herding village

near Amfissa, in the mountainous terrain of central Greece. He grew up tending his goats and craving the peaceful retreat of the religious life . . . that is, until World War II.

With the onslaught of Italian and German troops, Theo abandoned his desire for the cloth and approached the war with the same single-minded devotion he had reserved for the priesthood. He joined the underground, a country boy of sixteen.

It was in this context that he met Hawk, then a rising star in the newly formed firmament of the OSS. Hawk was coordinating the resistance effort in the Balkans, and he quickly became extremely impressed with the deadly talents of the "shepherd priest." It was Theo's very effectiveness that necessitated his removal from the Balkan theater. The Germans were pursuing him relentlessly, and Hawk felt Theo had talents that could be utilized elsewhere. He was sent back to England, and with the same keenness of mind that had enabled him to memorize the Bible by the age of six, he learned, in seven months, enough Portuguese to fool the locals.

His dark features and stocky peasant build enabled him to pass as native, and he took up the duties of the Lisbon station. Supposedly neutral Portugal was a hotbed of German espionage activity, and between Hawk's incisive training and Theo's own teen-age innocence, the Allies were amply rewarded with volumes of valuable intelligence.

Once the war had ended, Theo contemplated a return to the cloth. But there was too much blood on his hands, and too much of the world in his head, to allow it. Hawk seized the opportunity to return the boy to the States. Both of them struggled through the change-over as the wartime apparatus of the OSS evolved into the more permanent institution of the CIA.

But the CIA charter was just too restricting, and both

grew dissatisfied with the change.

It was Hawk and Theo together, working on their own to clean up several CIA mistakes, that finally convinced the powers that be that an organization of a more flexible—though more secret—design was called for.

AXE was born, and while Hawk ran the organization, Theo ran the agents, the godfather of the Killmaster Corps.

The man's image formed itself in my mind like a silent eulogy. At age fifty-six, still a marvel of physical strength, the man was a walking encyclopedia of espionage trade-craft. Ruggedly handsome, with features that only improved with age, he was a mixture of brilliance, arrogance, and vanity—a vanity that would not tolerate so much as a single gray hair on his own head. But if he was arrogant, it was from years of proving his abilities in the field.

Theo's departure was painful enough, but that he was alive and talking—a defector of the highest order—was downright agonizing.

I looked over at Hawk. He was staring intently at the crop of recruits below, his mind lost in some personal hell of his own enduring. He must have sensed my attention, because he pulled the cigar from his mouth and spoke.

"Yes, they'll *all* make it," he sighed, "and half of them won't live through their first assignments. Damn the bastard. Damn him!" Hawk stood abruptly and spat out an order in my direction. "Let's get out of here. This room is beginning to make me sick."

I followed the man out of the booth and down the hall to a series of offices marked *Research and Evaluation*. Hawk mumbled as he ushered me into the suite. "Had to change offices for a while, at least until we find out what the son-of-a-bitch is up to."

I noted once more the absence of Ginger Bateman

and questioned the man as we filed through into his temporary domain. I nearly crashed into him as he halted in his tracks. "She's in the infirmary. I came into the office Saturday afternoon and found her on the floor. He'd beaten the shit out of her."

"Is she okay?"

Hawk nodded. "Vocal cords are bruised up pretty bad, but other than that, she'll heal."

I winced at the thought of all that loveliness being abused. "Better give it to me from top to bottom."

Hawk stepped away and climbed behind his desk while I shut the door behind us. I settled into a chair of my own and prepared myself for the bad news. Hawk wasted no time in laying it out.

"Let's start at the beginning," he growled. "We're not the only ones with headaches. Theo never did anything without panache. He's walked out on us, all right, and he's taken one of the higher level ladies from Military Intelligence with him."

"What's her name?"

"Leslie Solari."

Although I'm not usually involved in military affairs, I do try to keep abreast of the various honchos of the sister groups. The name rang no bells.

"How high does she reach?" I asked.

"How does personal secretary to Number One himself grab you?" came the clipped reply.

Another jolt of pain washed over me. "Like you said, Theo's got panache. And I assume it's safe to conclude that she didn't elope without some kind of baggage. What did she take with her, and how bad are we hurting?"

Hawk's answering snort was totally humorless. "How right you are. She left in style, N3. She took with her every shred of information regarding U.S. and Allied nuclear capability and deployment, a regular Sears catalogue of American defenses."

"What's her connection with Theo?"

Another snort. "As far as we can see, it's purely rec-
reational. They've been dating for about a year. Word
from the boys at G-2 is that she's head over heels in love
with the bastard. It doesn't take too much imagination
to see how he's been using it."

"How'd they pull it off?"

"From what we can determine, they've been gathering the data for months but keeping it on the premises.
Then, Saturday, they made their move. Taking full advantage of the lighter security, and all of Ms. Solari's
credentials, they simply walked in and walked out, taking the whole package in one clean stroke. It wasn't until
Sunday that we found the bodies of two security guards.
They'd been garotted."

I paused a moment to light up one of my specially
blended cigarettes. "I imagine it's safe to assume our
defectors are long gone?"

Hawk nodded. "Free and clear. They made it out of
the country on the first international flight."

"You think they'll head behind the Iron Curtain?"

Hawk settled his elbows onto the desk. "No. That's
what's interesting. The goods aren't being peddled to
the Russians outright. As far as we've been able to determine, they headed for Portugal. They had to know
they'd be found out within the day. Portugal has a live-
and-let-live policy. They're on neutral ground, and considering Theo's World War II experience, familiar
ground at that."

"So what's the game?"

"As of now, we really don't know for sure. But
there's a pretty solid rumor beginning to simmer that the
information is going to be auctioned on the open market. Sold to the highest bidder."

I choked momentarily on my cigarette. "Are you telling me we could just buy the stuff back?"

Hawk shrugged. "If the rumor is true, yes."

I paused a moment to consider the implications. "My God," I sighed, "he's got it locked up. With info like that, you've got to assume half a billion on the opening bid alone. He'll come away with enough money to start his own nation—and he'll still have enough left over to hire a small army to protect it!"

Hawk nodded and clamped down—hard—on the stub of his cigar. "Clever bastard, ain't he?" he snorted.

"How have we been handling our losses?" I asked.

"Both ourselves and Military Intelligence are doing what we can to minimize the damage. I'm sure you noticed the chaos on your way in. Codes are being altered, offices relocated, schedules revamped, security tightened. The usual procedures. But that's just surface stuff. Military Intelligence can't very well alter their arsenal."

"And we can't notify our allies without generating wholesale panic, right?"

Hawk thrust a finger in my direction. "You got it. Military Intelligence has joined with the CIA in an all-out manhunt for the couple, but if you ask me, I doubt that they'll find either of them. Theo's just too damn good. If the rumor is true, I think they'll be content to buy back the goods and keep the embarrassment under their own brass hats."

"How do we stand?"

"Same as the khaki crowd. We're juggling the organization, but the odd feeling I get is that we really don't have to."

I flipped an ash into the tray on Hawk's desk. "I don't follow you."

"The organizational crap is just the surface. It's the kind of information Theo carries in his head. I honestly believe it's safe with him. He won't reveal any of it unless he has to. And, right now, he doesn't have to."

Hawk settled back in his chair as he continued.

"He's the best, N3. The CIA and Military Intelligence just don't have the combined smarts to nail him. They'll chase their own asses around in circles, then give up the second the material is auctioned back or the system is revamped."

The reality of Hawk's appraisal was anything but encouraging. "So, who the hell needs them?" I offered. "We'll do our own housecleaning."

Hawk's pause was long, and his voice, when he finally spoke, was weak. "We can't, Nick. The son-of-a-bitch has neutralized us."

Vague echoes of Hawk's statements in the observation room began to haunt me. Whatever events had come down over the weekend, I had the feeling the worst of it was yet to be revealed. I waited with apprehension as Hawk went on.

"No. What Theo's got in his head could hurt us, but it can't kill us. It's what was in my safe that was deadly."

"Tell me."

"I had a Saturday morning conference with the president. Theo knew it. No sooner had he and his lady friend cleaned out the Pentagon then they arrived here. Theo tried waltzing past Ginger on some pretext of having to log an agent evaluation. Somehow Ginger smelled it out and tried to stop him. She paid the price."

There was a surge of anger at the repeated image. "So will he," I stated.

The defiance in my voice seemed to offer Hawk some satisfaction. He nodded. "But there's more. It seems that during the months he was gathering the nuclear info, he was also selling bits and pieces of AXE. He knew all the past capers—just who the major offenders were, and those most offended. He sold out each agent in turn, any fragment of information that an angry enemy could want."

During the past hour, I'd seen Hawk display more emotion than in all the years I'd known him. Now the flesh around his collar grew red with anger as the words kept spilling out. "My guess is that he was rewarded with large sums of money, no doubt dropped quietly into any one of several Swiss institutions. He could offer them all the information they needed except for one thing: the current locations and schedules for agents in the field. I'm the only one who ever knows where the Killmaster Corps is functioning at any given moment."

The certainty of Hawk's next statement had already burned itself in my brain. The question was painful but had to be asked. "That is until Saturday, correct?"

Hawk lifted violently from his chair. "All too correct. I keep the information on current missions in my wall safe. The bastard walked right in and cleaned it out. He got the total rap sheet on all field agents—their whereabouts, their missions, the whole ball of wax!"

I leaped in my chair as Hawk's angry fist slammed down onto the desk. "Running money! That's what hurts. The man spends twenty-five years building an organization, then peddles it off for running money!"

Hawk held a moment and then stalked off to the window. I could see his arms shaking as the full tide of his emotions raged within him. I remained silent, interred with my own thoughts. When Hawk turned back, the fire had managed to drain from his face.

"Sorry," he muttered, jamming his cigar back into his mouth and moving back into his chair. "Anyway, he's got it, and I can only assume that every asshole with a personal bitch has got it too. The second I realized what he had done, I issued a Code-7."

The remembered images of N7 and N12 flashed

through my brain. Even against the pungent odor of Hawk's cigar, the smell of death was infecting my nostrils. Once more, the bony fingers were reaching far too close to home. My voice was quiet as I asked the inevitable question.

"How many have reported in?"

Hawk was just as solemn with his answer. "Three. Qualley, Darnell, and Baldrich." His eyes then floated up to embrace me. "And let's not forget you, Nick. Where the hell did you get to? I thought the bastard had nailed you too!"

I explained my weekend retreat as best I could, emphasizing the Mid-East deaths as my motive. In view of the circumstances, Hawk accepted the explanation without challenge.

"Some homecoming," he added ruefully.

I nodded and pushed the conversation on. "Do you think Theo will try for you? Is that what Qualley's doing in your office with your double?"

"A precaution; one that I think is probably unnecessary. In spite of events, Theo has some scruples. I don't think he'll sell *me* out. He worked too hard to help build AXE."

For a moment I could not believe my ears. "He has also, rather effectively, destroyed it."

Hawk's hand rose to correct me. "Neutralized, not destroyed. There's a difference. He's eliminated most of the agents, but not the organization. That's why I think the information he carries is safe. He won't expose us unless he has to, and right now, he doesn't have to."

The ingeniousness of the man suddenly hit me. "Christ," I hissed, "he's not only sold us out for running money, but he's also managed to eliminate the only group capable of matching him in the process. By killing us off, he's bought freedom from pursuit!"

Hawk's nod was a resigned one. "Unlike Military Intelligence, we've got no place to turn. We're secret—we work alone or we don't work at all. It'll take at least a year before we can rebuild a Killmaster Corps with the necessary skills and field experience to beat him.''

"And does he think we'll forget in that time?"

Hawk studied the desk top pensively. "Maybe. If not, he can always threaten us with what's in his head. We can survive the agent crisis, but exposure would bury us.''

A sudden rush of admiration streamed through me. "But you're going to try anyway, aren't you? That's what you were doing down at the observation booth."

Hawk showed the glimmer of a smile. "I never was a good loser. I was trying to find candidates for reprisal. Then you walked in."

I returned the smile. "I'm here, sir. Alive and kicking. What would you like me to do?"

Whatever negativity had been festering in the room vanished with the soothing salve of activity. Hawk leaped into the task of assigning me.

"Obviously, your first priority is the nuclear information. Check out the auction rumors. Buy it back, steal it, destroy it—whatever you have to do to keep it from enemy hands. Price is no object.''

I doused my cigarette in the ashtray. "What about the other buyers? They won't take too kindly to being overbid.''

Hawk discounted my question with a shake of his hoary head. "Theo's running the show. He won't let anyone renege. He'll run a clean auction, with airtight security insurance. I don't think the other buyers will have any choice in the matter.''

"And just what is it you want me to do with Theo?"

A fire passed quickly across Hawk's eyes. "Although I'm guessing the information is safe with Theo, I don't think we can afford to risk it. In my estimation, he's unsalvageable. I recommend immediate field termination."

I nodded my agreement. "I rather guessed you would. What about the girl?"

"I don't imagine Military Intelligence is feeling any more charitable than we are."

Again I nodded, then rose to go. Hawk's voice halted me.

"Be careful, N3. I don't have to tell you who you're working against. What makes it all the worse is that you're going to have to do it on your own. We can't offer you any support. Whoever he's sold your dossier to will know every safe-house, every travel route, every bit of possible AXE cover we could offer. It's my opinion you stand a better chance by working solo."

I smiled. "No problem. I'll just hunt down one of the best agents I've ever known—the man who taught me the craft—and dodge assassins' bullets at the same time. Who needs cover?"

Hawk rose from his seat and extended his hand. I gripped it firmly. Then an involuntary chuckle escaped my lips. Hawk's eyebrows furrowed in confusion.

"Just thinking of a line I once heard in a movie," I explained. "It was called *Baltimore Bullet*. This pool hustler had to play his protégé for the championship. The protégé was agonizing the hell out of himself because he was so sure he was going to beat his teacher. The teacher solved the dilemma in one quick phrase."

"What was that?"

" 'You're good, kid. I taught you everything you know . . . but I *didn't* teach you everything *I* know!' "

For one brief second, Theo hung in the room like a ghost.

# THREE

I was twenty minutes out of London's Heathrow Airport, and the Atlantic lay stretched out beneath the plane like an icy gray carpet. The sun was cascading in the port side, and there was not so much as a hint of a cloud to disturb the vista below. But my mood was more in harmony with the chilling waters than the burning sun.

"Excuse me, Father, can I get you a drink?"

I turned to answer the voice, unsure for a moment that I was the target of her comment. A Portuguese stewardess stared down at me, her plastered-on smile a bit more heartfelt in response to my garb. Although my body would have been more delighted by a double Chivas, I responded as befitted my station.

"How sweet of you, my dear. Yes, please. A glass of port would be wonderful."

She bustled off down the aisle, my admiring eyes a silent companion. Her firm little behind, testing to the limit the stitching of her airline pantsuit, did much to soothe the darkness of my thoughts. I settled back and did my best to retain the mood.

The three days since my encounter with Hawk were

31

not without some cause for hope.

I had spent most of that Monday afternoon helping out around the complex. There was no point in going back to my apartment until the bomb squad had given it the okay. I utilized the time to pay a short visit to Ginger Bateman in her infirmary bed.

Once I had managed to forget the bruises that covered her face and arms, and once I had gotten used to the hoarse whispering tone of her voice, I was quite delighted with the visit. Ginger's relief at the mere fact of my being alive was more than heartwarming. As the visit progressed, the optimism and pure Southern grit of her nature did much to still whatever doubts I may have had. She did her best to shower me with all the positive energy her infirmity would allow.

Just watching her try—each word she spoke a visible effort through bruised vocal cords—was all the commitment I needed. I would make Theo pay. That was a promise!

By the time I rejoined Hawk, the momentum of events had begun their course. The bomb squad had combed the apartment and deemed it "clean." But where they failed to find incendiaries, they did find something else. Upon entry, they had stumbled onto three men.

One of the men had made a rather unfortunate mistake. He had opened my weekend suitcase. While the blast had apparently tossed it around, Samsonite made good on their claims, and the bag had survived undamaged. What had not survived was Pierre, my tiny, rounded gas bomb.

I don't usually take weekend retreats armed to the teeth, but AXE does expect a certain caution from their stable of agents. A Killmaster makes too many enemies to ever feel totally secure. My concession to safety is to

take my weaponry along, but relegate it to the more appropriate atmosphere of my bag. Under field condi-
tions, Pierre would ride proudly, mounted to my
crotch—a third bauble in the Carter family jewels.

But in this instance, he had traveled along in the suitcase. As a result of the blast, Pierre had broken open,
the lethal potential of his vapors held in check until the
unfortunate search and release by the stranger. The
man probably never even knew what took him.

What was fortunate was that the bomb squad chose
that moment to enter. The other two men fled before
they had the opportunity to either remove or strip the
body. As a result, the bomb squad could return with full
identification on the intruder: Manoel Delvao; resi-
dence: Oporto, Portugal.

Much to my relief, they also returned with the suitcase's two survivors: Wilhelmina and Hugo. Wilhelmina
is my pride and joy, a 9mm Luger that has proven more
faithful than any sainted lady. And where Wilhelmina
cannot go, Hugo can. Hugo is a pencil-thin stiletto, usually concealed in a chamois sheath on my forearm. With
one quick slap against my thigh, he will drop into my
hand, ready for whatever demands I make upon him.

While Pierre is replaceable from the AXE storehouse
of arms, I would feel quite a bit more naked without the
friendly feel of my other two pals. I thanked the squad
leader as he departed.

Hawk and I then settled in to discuss strategy. The
fact that the apartment had been checked put a slight
crimp in our plans. We had hoped to convince the world
that I was dead. That would serve to take the pressure of
dodging assassins' bullets off my back. But the two men
who had escaped would no doubt inform their boss of
the blast's failure.

I was still among the hunted.

What is more, the apartment itself would no doubt be watched in case I returned. Hawk decided I would have to bypass the luxury of packing up, and go "as I was." He took it even one step further by demanding that I make my departure from AXE via the secret tunnel that connected the Amalgamated building with nearby R Street.

AXE might be watched too.

Hawk set it up with all the finesse befitting the craft. A dummy vehicle was dispatched from the front entry with a Nick Carter look-alike at the wheel. I then stalled, exited through the tunnel, and joined an unmarked car waiting to pick me up. I was driven straight to Fort George G. Meade and dumped aboard a military flight to New York City. While I winged my way north, Hawk phoned ahead to arrange for bogus documentation, all through very un-AXE-like channels.

Monday night was spent in conference with Willie Gies, New York's number one makeup artist. Willie is my own secret resource, unknown to the powers at AXE, and I wanted to keep it that way. We met in a tiny restaurant in the Village, our cabal clothed in secrecy.

Willie ate it up; it was his chance to play spy.

Willie is very gay, and from his usual appearance you know he doesn't give a damn who knows it. I wouldn't have been surprised if he'd shown up for our "secret meeting" in a gold lamé trenchcoat and rhinestone-studded shades. Tonight, however, well-tailored Christopher St. casual won out over glitter.

But whatever subtlety the man often lacked in his own life, he's always an artist when it comes to providing it for others. I explained my needs as generally as I could and awaited the man's suggestions. The result was the priestly clothing I now wore, right down to the collar, beard, and X ray-proof, hollowed-out Bible that guaranteed safe passage for my weaponry.

The irony of the choice—especially in view of Theo's past religious leanings—did not escape me. Nor did it deter me.

Tuesday was spent in the costume's construction, and Hawk initiated paperwork to back it up. Father Larry O'Hanlon was being born. That night, the good Father—with God undoubtedly at his side—hopped the first commercial flight for London.

With AXE blown, cover had to be sought elsewhere, and Wednesday was spent obtaining it. Britain's MI-6 has always proven a steady ally, and they continued to live up to their status. I appealed to Davidson Harcourt, one of British Intelligence's most able leaders and a man I am proud to consider a friend. I leveled with him, giving him the entire picture, and he responded by immediately withdrawing two of his top field operatives and ordering them from their current position in South Africa to the more northerly clime of Portugal. His assurance that both hotel and team would be awaiting my arrival in Lisbon was a relief to a beleaguered soul.

His hospitality extended even further, with the offer of a full night's sleep at one of London's more elegant safe-houses. By the next morning, Father O'Hanlon was safely tucked and secured into his Lisbon-bound flight, God still at his side.

At the moment, God found himself dodging the approaching elbow of the stewardess.

"Here you are, Father. I hope you enjoy it."

I smiled my most beneficent smile and accepted the glass. I stared into her liquid eyes and struggled with thoughts of a more carnal nature. As a whole, the Portuguese are not a particularly beautiful people. They are generous to a fault and kind without reservation, but the women don't usually turn me on.

This stewardess was the exception that proved the rule. She was Manueline architecture at its finest. I gripped her hand a moment and leaned into her with a conspiratorial whisper.

"Listen, my dear. I don't know if this"—I nodded at the glass in my hand—"will help. I don't take too well to flying."

Her Catholic background brought a small hint of shock to her face, but her liberal nature smiled. "Why, Father, don't you put your trust in God?"

I nodded vehemently. "I've spent my life with God. I trust him completely. It's the pilot I've never met!"

She giggled, winked, and wiggled off toward her station. Her return was swift and appreciated. She slipped me a small miniature, then departed with yet another wink. "Better than the wine, yes?" she grinned.

"God bless," I grinned back.

I did my damnedest to enjoy the miniature of scotch as I began putting things together in my mind. The situation, at the moment, required reflection. Later it would require skill and courage.

My first chore was to break down the bombing attempt. That keys had been copied, lock sequences broken, and security bypassed was no longer a mystery in the light of N1's defection.

The insider had become the outsider.

Theo had sold out almost every agent he had ever groomed—all but four. That even four survived was pure luck. Darnell and Baldrich had made it only because they had been involved in a joint AXE/CIA seminar program, and were safe within the confines of Langley.

Qualley had survived on pure luck. He had gone out Friday night hunting for hookers—and had found them.

He had gotten so drunk that one of them had to drive him home. He had been preparing to go reclaim his car on Saturday when the Code-7 had come in. He had cabbed his way—as duty demanded—to Dupont Circle. It was the Amalgamated messenger who went to claim his vehicle for him that suffered Qualley's intended fate. The car was wired, and the poor kid was scattered over the entire block.

My own survival had been a combination of luck and skill, a marriage of elements that left a hollow echo bouncing around inside my guts. There was a paradox in the near-miss bomb attempt that haunted me.

On the one hand was the rather basic and rudimentary rigging of the Glenlivet bottle. Combined with that was the careless handling of the bedroom door that first aroused my suspicions. Once I had been tipped—a sloppy oversight at best—discovering the trigger had been merely a process of elimination.

Whomever Theo had sold me to would know everything that Theo knew about me. If the assassin knew enough of my personality to wire the scotch bottle, he would also have to know my abilities. The bomb should have been rigged carefully, with the fullest attention to detail. After all, I was not expecting it. Fresh from a weekend away, I was a sitting duck. I had no way of knowing that AXE had been breached.

In spite of this, the door had been left open and the bomb found.

But, on the other hand, a secondary trip had been mounted in the elevator. Very unexpected . . . very sophisticated. How was I to interpret the contrast?

I had a very hazy profile on my killer. He was either very careless, or he was very clever. The open door and the traditional wiring had either been an oversight of the highest order—or an arrogant taunt. Which was it?

The realization slammed into me like a knife.

The killer might be sloppy, but Theo was not. The bomb was no doubt the assassin's idea; the elevator trigger, Theo's. The picture began to clear.

Although my assassin was not so smart, he was being guided by someone who was. The key, if one was to be found, would be in following the mistakes, not the panache or ingenuity. I stored that into my think tank for future retrieval.

But just who was it that I was dodging?

I recalled Hawk's comment from the briefing: *He knew all the past capers—just who the major offenders were, and those most offended.* In light of this, it seemed very likely that I would have to know my pursuer. The aftermath had been audited, and at least one of the men doing the checking was a Portuguese national.

But was he? Was my tormentor a Portuguese? Or was he merely hiring Portuguese talent?

I wracked my brains trying to come up with anyone I may have offended—by word or deed—in Portugal. The list, when it finally formed, was slim indeed. Portugal was hardly the hotbed of intrigue that it had been in World War II. If one was going to find "those most offended," one would have to search elsewhere for the prime candidates. So why a Portuguese assassin?

The think tank spat itself back at me with lightning efficiency. Don't look for motive in the killer; look instead at the killer's source.

Theo!

For a moment, I tried to put myself in N1's recently departed shoes. If I were to defect, as Theo had, how would I handle it?

The Killmaster Corps—at least those that I had known—flashed through my brain. Many could be discounted. Although all the Corps—any of those who bear the distinction of Killmaster—are factors to be considered with awe, they are only judged so by the enemy. To someone of Theo's caliber, there are only a certain few who deserve extreme consideration.

Were I to defect, were I to sell out the only men who could nail me, there would only be a group of about ten agents I would handle with kid gloves. The others could be taken with relative ease.

I put myself into Theo's place and thought it through.

Of the men I considered to be real threats to my treachery, two had been eliminated in the Middle East fiasco that had been the basis of my weekend flight. That left eight. Of the eight, six were on sensitive missions. If I were going to compromise them, I had only to inform the parties they were investigating to gain the desired result. An exposed agent is a dead agent.

That left only two agents of noteworthy caliber. Though neither were on active missions, both had been on permanent station: one in Poland and one in Turkey. Permanent station meant known territory, meant nonmobility, and meant easy elimination. One had only to hand out addresses, and the agents involved would be as helpless as parakeets in a cage.

That leaves only . . . me.

Fantasy is a device pleasurable in its execution. In mine, *I* was the defector. That left no one. But in Theo's mind, I was the only reality left to be dealt with. How was I to be accounted for? I was neither on current loan, nor was I on permanent station.

Click! Ding! The thoughts fell into place.

I am no longer the villain. I am the hero. I am someone Theo has to account for. How does he do it? If he knows he is going to be spending his time in Portugal, he sells his one uneliminated hero to a local. And if the assassin is sloppy—if the man is not too bright—Theo would make damn sure that any possibility of failure was covered where I was concerned.

If the first attempt failed, he would make certain that I would chase *him*, as I most certainly would, through every inch of the assassin's home territory.

Theo, you may be a shit, but you're the best shit in the business!

Assassin profile? Not too efficient, but guided. Someone I *may* know, but not one of the prime offenders in my career. He is Portuguese, but not necessarily involved in the hubbub of international affairs. He knows he missed on the first go-round, but he also knows I am beelining straight into his own nest. He will exist in close proximity to the man I am really concerned with: Theo. Of that I was certain.

Realization brings with it a certain comfort. Knowledge can be acted on. Uncertainty is the killer.

I began putting the pieces together in my head. I would aim for the assassin first, staying underground in the process. No matter how well he was guided, the assassin himself had flaws. He could be persuaded, or coerced, to end the hunt. If he was truly arrogant, he could slip up. But if the failure was the result of actual incompetence, he would fall. I would see to it.

That left only the possible auction, and the eventual location of Theo and his girl, to deal with. For this, at least at the moment, I would have to rely on the confidence and direction of Davidson Harcourt and his MI-6 team. I could do a hell of a lot worse.

But what of the eventual confrontation?

I may be one of AXE's best—the fact that I'm still alive would indicate I must be doing *something* right—but was Theo better? He was, after all, the teacher.

Legend has it that the best teachers are measured by the number of students that surpass them. But does the same apply in this case?

He taught me all I know. Did he teach me everything that *he* knew in the process?

Facing Theo would test every shred of skill and confidence I possessed. It was the ultimate face-off. Was I up to it? Did I have what it took to take down one of my own?

The question lingered in my mind. But before I could frame an answer, my thoughts were intruded on by a familiar voice.

"Pardon me, Father. But I think I'm in sudden need of absolution."

I turned to greet the comment, but found myself cut short. Although the voice was familiar, the face was not. More accurately, the face was recognizable but totally devoid of the fifty-odd years that should have been registered upon it.

I offered my greeting weakly. "Countess?"

Her laughter was all the confirmation I required. "Really, Nicholas! How gauche! Is it *that* noticeable?"

She settled herself down into the seat next to me. It was then that I became aware that the body was no less rejuvenated than the face. I knew the countess to be in her fifties, but the woman that was now displaying herself to me could easily have passed for thirty-five.

"Are you through?" she smirked.

I finally gained control of my senses. "I—I'm sorry, Countess. It's just that it's a little mind-boggling. I've never had anyone change on me like that."

She smiled and laid a conspiratorial hand on my arm. "I know. It's a marvelous age we live in. My mother spent her life bathing in oils and coating herself with creams, and she still ended up looking like a prune. If Russia had discovered plastic surgery, the Revolution would have shriveled up and blown away!"

I smiled inwardly at the mention of her heritage. Countess Irena Voslovich had spent a lifetime building her own myth. Both of her parents had supposedly been White Russian émigrés, children of the aristocracy fleeing the Russian civil war of 1918. They had grown up in exile in Germany during the twenties, met, married, and given birth to the proud lady next to me. Her father had gotten involved with the Krupp works but soon deserted to form his own armaments empire. His constant travels and contacts with the mighty were Irena's schooling, polish, and the source of the power she now possessed in the world's arms bazaar.

It was a legend befitting the international élan of the lady herself. She was a blend of ruthlessness and charm that made her both the scourge and the prima hostess of Europe. She was also as phony as a four dollar bill.

In the years I had known her, I had come to learn bits and pieces of the real story. Her grandparents had indeed been Russian immigrants, a Jewish family escaping the pogroms. Her parents had met and married in the Manhattan ghetto they called home. Irena had entered the world with the name Sarah Blatsky, but she was blessed with all the beauty the Good Lord could spare.

She used that beauty to snare the affections of a local mobster, but she was forced to flee New York when a family war threatened to end her life. She sailed off to Europe; her hubby never made it. Once in Europe, it was those same looks that caught the eye of Ivan Voslovich, a small-time arms pusher.

The union was blessed. Between Sarah Blatsky's Lower East Side sense of what constitutes a good deal, her gangland-fostered street sense, and Ivan's complete acceptance of her dominating nature, the business grew into the empire it now was. With "Countess Irena" tutoring Ivan every step of the way, the aristocratic myth was born, and Europe responded. One hates to buy one's arms from commoners.

"Enough of me," chimed the Countess. "I'm beautiful and I know it. What of you? Why are you on this *dreary* flight to *dreary* old Portugal, and why the hell do you look like a fugitive from *The Bells of Saint Mary's*?"

My answer was simple. "Business . . . you understand."

There was no doubt she would. As well as selling the Third World—or any world—its arms, Irena's contacts with the world's elite made her privy to information. It was part of the dual nature of the lady that she would occasionally sell that information for the right price. While arms were her vocation, espionage was her hobby, and she was a free-lancer of the highest order.

Her eyebrow arched, a note of interest struck in the darker corners of her personality. While her face may have hinted at interest, she was far too smooth to allow her voice the same luxury.

"Business, indeed," she scoffed. Her hand came up and tugged at a few hairs of the beard on my face. Several came loose, suffered her appraisal, and then drifted to the floor as she cast them away. "Nicholas, *really!* You're much too old to be playing these silly games."

In spite of her blatant disregard of my secrecy, I was forced to smile. "It keeps me young. Some of us have surgeons, some of us 'controls.' "

She dismissed the dig with a wave of her bejeweled hand. "Foolishness. You should work for me, you lovely boy. Then you could be wearing suits, not cheap disguises. Look at me. Am I forced to travel like the Virgin Mary?"

While my eyes responded, my mind clicked into gear. Was this a business trip? And if it were, could it possibly involve the auction of the nuclear arsenal? There was only one way to find out.

"You're lovely, as always, Countess. And what

brings *you* to dreary old Portugal?"

Her eyes held me suspiciously for a moment. Then a smile broke out over her creamy face. "Business . . . you understand!"

I nodded, acknowledging the competitiveness of her nature. The woman would reveal nothing on her own. If I was going to get information of the auction, it would not be volunteered. I took a different tack. If you want a truth confirmed, assume it to be true yourself.

"We wouldn't happen to be going on the same business, would we?"

Her defenses bristled. "I really wouldn't know, dear boy. Just what is your business?"

I stared thoughtfully out the window. The coast of Portugal could be seen looming up from below. I allowed the edge to build and then turned back to her. "As you said before, Countess. I'm getting a little old for this game. I've been thinking of changing careers. I heard a rumor that there are arms for sale. Like you, I think it's time I started traveling first class."

A glimmer of recognition sparkled in her eyes. I noted it and raised my hand in mock concern. "I'm not thinking of competing, you understand. No small arms. I wouldn't want to tread on your territory. This is slightly bigger stuff. Long-range goods. No competition. You understand?"

The response was there, hidden behind a cold mask of reserve and caution, but there. She studied me a moment, then patted my arm once more. The smile she gave me was tight, her voice held mocking warmth.

"You naïve little creature. *Everyone* is competition."

Bingo! Confirmed. The auction was on. The question now was, where?

"Well, dear child," she said lightly, "I really must get back to Gustav. He's a brilliant aide but a lousy drinker. If his Prussian blood gets up, I'm afraid they may chuck him out the cargo hatch. Do keep in touch. I see you far too seldom."

She stood up and started toward the first class section, but a quick grip of her wrist halted her. "Listen, Countess, I'm kind of new at this arms racket. I was wondering if you might be willing to give me some advice. Who knows . . . maybe we can even combine resources?"

What had started as a gripping of her wrist had evolved into a tender, sensual massage. Her eyes floated down to watch my gesture. When they returned to my face, they were lit with a natural excitement. "Why, thank you, Father. That would be lovely. Perhaps we could get together in Lisbon."

"Sounds heavenly," I grinned.

"You'll find me at the Ritz, of course. Say tomorrow . . . around one o'clock? Make it a light lunch?"

I nodded. " 'Til then, may God be with you."

She released herself gently from my grasp and chuckled, then leaned down to whisper, "Better He stay with you, Father. He's a bore at parties, and He just can't close a deal!" With a quick wave, she was gone.

I settled back into my seat and clicked on my seat belt as the light flicked on overhead. Below me lay Lisbon, the red-tiled roofs shimmering in the bright sunshine. I downed the last of my drink and returned it to the stewardess. My mood was oddly buoyant.

I turned again to the window, the sprawling layout of Lisbon rising up to welcome me. Somewhere in that fascinating city of hills and cobblestone streets was a man who was waiting to kill me. Somewhere else, a man to be killed. The assassin would be dealt with, but what of the assassination? Could I beat the best?

As if for an answer, I turned to the vacant seat next to me. I studied the emptiness. Something had changed.

God was no longer at my side.

# FOUR

*For whoever wishes to save his life shall lose it; but whoever loses his life for my sake and the gospel's shall save it.*

Mark 8:35.

I am not a religious man; in my business it's hard to be. But I do have an intimate concern with Fate, and I wondered now why she had chosen this particular morsel to catch my eye. The words on the page blurred, and an image of Hawk formed itself on the back of my eyelids. *Whoever loses his life for my sake . . . shall save it.*

I shrugged to dispel the chill the words were causing.

My perusal was not for enjoyment or edification. It was strictly business. The Bible's X ray shielding had gotten my weaponry through TWA's security in New York, and Harcourt had gotten me through England's. But this was Portugal, and there was no guarantee that one of the customs men would not become unduly curious of my literature, priestly clothing or not.

It was a testimony to Willie Gies's genius that the hollowed-out section that contained Wilhelmina and Hugo was restricted to the Old Testament: Exodus through Malachi. This enabled me to open the book to certain legitimate sections without revealing my wares. A customs official would be far more suspicious of a closed book than an open one.

I waited until only five people stood before me in line before flipping open the book and eyeing Fate's taunting verse. I then read on, doing my best to fill my face with appropriate rapture. The brilliance of my performance was upstaged only by the sudden burst of a female voice from across the counters.

I looked up to see the Countess in heated debate with one of the guards. Next to her stood a chunky, dwarfish, bespectacled figure that I assumed to be Gustav, her aide. The two were waging a verbal battle with the customs man, a battle that seemed a draw until the timely appearance of the chief customs agent.

The customs boss took one look at the regal beauty, recognized her, and joined *her* team in a verbal assault upon the poor guard. With visions of transfer to the Spanish border plaguing his mind, the guard backed off and gestured Gustav and his cartload of baggage blithely through. Her mission successful, the Countess remained to reconcile the frightened guard and his master.

I couldn't help but smirk at the scene. I felt a touch of envy at her first class status, a status I usually possess myself. But there was also admiration. While I was creeping through customs fearing for my Bible, she had just waltzed nine bags—containing Lord knows what kind of deviltry—smack under the noses of Portugal's best.

Her complete control was evident in the now smiling faces of the two officials as they shook her hands in supplication. The scene was marred only by the sudden outburst of another bit of upstaging to my right.

I turned to look, grateful to find my place in line reduced to third. But my own confrontation with customs was being delayed by the upstager himself.

He was native and obviously suffering from one too many scotches on his own flight. He was yelling at the customs guard, his Portuguese slurred and rapid, complaining that the airline had lost his luggage. Although the guard was doing his best to shuffle the man off to the baggage department, the drunk seemed unable to grasp the logic of the man's suggestion.

Progress came to a standstill and a small crowd began to gather, when I suddenly felt the stinging awareness of eyes. I looked back toward the Countess and found her staring at me. The look in her eyes was as undefinable as the woman herself. It possessed a fire that bordered on the sexual, but it was the kind of fire one gets from the successful anticipation of a business deal, or the successful elimination of an enemy.

She left me to answer the question as she turned and spoke once more to the man who ran customs. I felt an icy chill creep through me as she muttered to the man, her hand gesturing blatantly in my direction.

I tensed. The sadistic side of the Countess's nature, the competitive instincts that delighted in the kill, began to weigh heavily on my mind. As I stood now, I was vulnerable. I had offered her a deal, and she had led me to believe she was interested.

But that was the Countess's peculiar talent. She could be Queen Victoria, winning your confidence with hors d'oeuvres on a silver platter, and then be the Marquis de Sade, feeding you your own skull for the main course.

She had only to expose me—to hint, by truth or lies—that I was more than I seemed, and my weapons would be discovered, open Bible or not. Then, while I battled the authorities of Portugal, she would taste the delights of Lisbon: the auction and its goods her sole property.

The hapless guard she had so recently bilked was now standing at my shoulder, his hand tapping me. Slowly I closed the Bible, my finger sliding into the stiffened page that marked the section with my gun. I would test her loyalty, but I was prepared, if necessary, to blast my way into Lisbon.

He led me off toward his boss. The customs chief watched me every step of the way, his eyes cold and uncommunicative. Not even my understanding of the language could soften his stare. He asked politely for my passport, studied it, and stamped it, his face bursting into sudden glee. He gestured toward the retreating back of the Countess as he spoke.

"She asked, specifically, that you be hurried through. You have friends in high places."

Gesturing to the Bible, I answered with a smile, "I know."

The man's face collapsed. "Forgive me! I did not mean . . ."

But I cut him off with a fatherly "God bless" and made a beeline for the nearest cab stand. The Countess had come through. The confirmation of the more positive side of her nature left me with high hopes for the meeting to take place the next day. I silently thanked her also for saving me from the inebriated rantings of the misplaced baggage man.

As I departed, my eyes flew back to the counter to see if the dilemma had resolved itself. The crowd had dispersed, and the drunk was gone. Solely out of curiosity, I looked back toward the baggage section to see if the fight was waging there. I found the drunk.

But not where, or how, he should have been.

He was halfway back, loitering in the recess before one of the men's rooms. As my eyes caught his, he averted his gaze and stumbled back out into the main hall. He looked around in customary confusion, then scratched his head, muttered to himself, and started up toward me. By this time, I had turned back on my own course.

I had seen all I needed to.

In the second our eyes had met, two things had registered with clarity: one—no matter how much the man was staggering, the eyes had been crystal clear; and two—those eyes were not only quite sober, they were familiar. I knew him. Not recently, and not well. But I knew him.

And he knew me.

Chalk one up for Theo and Company.

The setup inked itself onto my brain with indelible certainty. The man behind me was the spotter, a killer too, perhaps, but primarily there to point me out. That meant there were others: strictly killers, all.

There were any number of ways to enter Portugal, and Theo would no doubt account for each. But the easiest and quickest would be flying in under cover. The assassin had merely to locate someone who knew me— someone who had personal experience—and sit him down over a series of drawings that covered my face through every possible method of disguise, then turn him loose in the airport. Finding such a man would be no problem. Theo knew all the past capers.

Once the spotter had sighted his quarry, he would point him out. Nothing blatant, mind you, not for our Theo. The man does not just rush up and stick his finger in my face. He waits until I am at a given point in the customs line, say fifth or third. He then does something specific, like approaching the guard or starting a drunken brawl, and the killers merely count down to me. Bingo! Their quarry is in a trap.

Spotting, however, is one thing; taking me down is another.

It's the crackpots and terrorists that crave the limelight. The assassin prefers the anonymity of silent, discreet removal, and the joy of living to "kill another day." Try taking me in the open, and you've got a fight on your hands. Try blasting me, and you've got an audience.

But catch me in line while my mind is bent on getting through, start the kind of diversion guaranteed to attract a crowd, slip a man in to my right and left, and suddenly we find yours truly kissing the linoleum with two stilettos sticking from his back.

As the confusion dies down, the killers slip off. And then, when the focus of activity begins revolving around the priestly body bleeding on the floor, who is going to take time out to challenge the drunken stranger weaving his way out of the airport?

Neat, Theo, very neat. But I'm neater.

The planning was brilliant, but it had all folded on account of the Countess's charity. I had been pulled from the jaws of death by the accommodating customs chief. That left the killers on their own.

My guess was that there were three. The spotter, Mr. Left, and Mr. Right. The first move was to cut down the odds.

I searched the hall, found the first men's room I could see, and stepped into it. Although the killers might be stupid, they were no doubt warned. They would know my abilities. In spite of the continuation of his drunken charade, the spotter knew I had caught him. It wouldn't do for him to be seen coming from one bathroom only to jump right into another. I was betting he would confer with his comrades and station himself on the outside . . . to ward off visitors, if nothing else.

I was cutting the opposition to two.

Once in the bathroom, my pace accelerated. There were three stalls. I ran to the first and stepped inside, latching the door behind me. As quickly as I could, I removed my pants and shoes. I raised the toilet seat and pinned the beltline of my trousers beneath it. I then kneeled and positioned my shoes as though I were sitting down. I bunched the trouser legs around the shoes, and pinned the excess back between the seat and the porcelain bowl. The final touch was to remove Hugo and Wilhelmina from their Biblical nest, and place the book neatly on the floor.

When the killers came looking for ankles, they would see nothing more threatening than a squatting priest, his attention on graffiti instead of the Holy Book.

My next step was to climb the outside wall of the partition and drop myself back into the room. I then hurried over to the last stall in the line. I latched it behind me and took up the same position as my clothing. A second pair of shoes would have been nice but wasn't available. My only hope was that when it came time for the killers to check out ankles, a pair of bare feet, in a country as poor as Portugal, would not strike them as too out of key.

I tucked Wilhelmina into the pocket of my coat. I could afford the noise of gunfire only as a last resort. Hugo nestled in my hand, his blade gleaming like the spotless tiles that surrounded me. My grip stiffened as the first sound of humanity entered the room.

The footfalls were random and tentative. Two men . . . right on, Carter! If I was as right about the quality of my assailants as I was about their numbers, I was in fat city. If my assassin and his crew were as textbook as I assumed them, the scenario would work itself out just as I had forced it on them.

The nervous shuffles and movements were muted confirmation of my strategy.

First came the cracking of a knee joint. The floor was

being scanned. Then came the rustles of clothing as the scanner rose. There was the faintest breath of a whispered conversation. The priest/spy had been found, but there was a second pair of ankles in the last booth.

I didn't doubt the ultimate resolution of the dilemma. The barefoot occupant of stall three could be overlooked. If the kill was silent, the extra party would never know it. If not, the killers would rely on the initial shock, and then terror, to keep the man in stall three from being too eager to greet the unknown. By that time the killers would be long gone.

That left only the deadly concerns of confessional number one.

Another exchange of whispers. My inability to hear was no hindrance to my understanding. They were debating their attack. For both to rush the booth door was foolish. If the door did not give, I would be warned. Worse, the two men would be together, creating only one direction for me to concentrate on. The best strategy would be to separate and come at me from two directions. If one of them failed, the other would not.

Once more, confirming footsteps. One of the men walked to the far side of the first stall. No good, Charlie! Nothing to stand on. That left only the center stall, because the toilet could be used to get over the intended victim. The footsteps followed even as I thought. The center booth was now occupied.

I bent down to watch the feet. The man took an upright position in front of the toilet, but the foot closest to me—the one that would not be visible from the first booth—lifted and rested itself on the wooden seat. The man awaited only his compadre's rush for the stall door to make his move.

The enemy was divided; it was time they be conquered.

As quietly as possible, I raised my own feet and lifted them onto my own toilet. I began to rise slowly, my body hugging the partition closest to my target. As my legs straightened, my body bent forward, keeping my head from appearing above the separation. Hugo found his way into my right hand.

The outside man made his move. He slammed into the stall door, and though it gave an agonized screech, it did not give. This was incidental to the man next to me. At the first sound of action, the man leaped onto the seat and lunged toward the open space above the first booth.

His body jolted twice. Once at the surprise of encountering the absence of life. Once at his loss of it.

As *he* moved, *I* moved, grabbing him by the hair and yanking him back toward me. Hugo entered his skull just behind the ear. With a few quick turns of my wrist, the cerebellum was mutilated, thereby destroying all motor functions. The man jerked erratically and then sank.

By the time my first charge was sinking, the man on the outside had made his way through the stall door. With a violent shattering of wood and formica, the barrier collapsed. The second assailant burst in and froze at the tableau of pants and porcelain. By the time he could even begin to grasp the implications, I was behind him.

Like shooting fish in a barrel.

The man jerked, turned, and realized his coming demise. He was hemmed in by the very booth he had negotiated. There was no room for finesse. He dropped his dagger and reached his hand desperately for the inside of his coat. He never made it.

With only a flick of my wrist, Hugo sailed the few feet that separated us and embedded himself in the killer's throat. There was a thin whistling sound that soon stilled itself as blood began bubbling through the rupture, and then he collapsed, joining his comrade in a grim, final ablution.

That left only the spotter on the outside.

The man knew my face. He would not greet it kindly when it emerged from the facilities. I needed a second or two of delay to get to him. I studied the man before me as I struggled for my gimmick. The blood was dripping down the front of his shirt and spattering onto Father O'Hanlon's pants.

I didn't worry about the soiling of my disguise. Father O'Hanlon had gone down the tubes the second he was spotted. But clothes of some sort, without telltale blood, were definitely in order. The idea chimed like a clock. Not only could I walk out in bloodless array, but I could buy the precious seconds necessary to get close to the man outside.

I moved back to the center booth and studied my first victim. There had been some bleeding from behind the ear, but most of it had settled into the fabric of his turtleneck sweater. As quickly as possible, I stripped the man, then I moved back to the sink area and prepared to dispose of my own clothes. It was hardly the kind of burial Father O'Hanlon would have ordered, but it worked. I stepped to the section where paper towels were disposed of and liberated the plastic liner in the can.

I reclaimed pants, shoes, and Bible from the first stall, and relegated all but the shoes to their coffin. The coat, shirt, and collar joined. I then slipped on the killer's trousers, my own shoes, and with a little bit of plastic surgery—the kind even the Countess would have praised—the turtleneck became a V-neck. With the addition of the jacket, all was in readiness.

I moved to the entry and peered out cautiously.

Through the faint crack in the door I could see my spotter pacing the alcove. I closed the door, tucked Wilhelmina into my pocket, stuck Hugo in my teeth, gripped my plastic bag firmly, and backed out of the bathroom.

The spotter bought the ruse. Having only my back to refer to, he accepted the familiar clothing and similar build as that of his accomplice. I was no more than five paces from the door when I felt his hand touch my shoulder.

The second it did, I dropped the remains of Father O'Hanlon and gripped the offending appendage. With a quick turn of body, and a quicker turn of wrist, three of his fingers broke cleanly and quietly. The man's eyes went wide in pain and realization. Before the mounting scream could erupt, my left hand was covering his mouth, and my right hand was pressing Hugo into his ribs.

I pushed him to the far wall of the alcove and stared into his ashen face. "You're a dead man, you know that?" I hissed in Portuguese.

The eyes that hovered and darted above my palm were sick with understanding. The head nodded weakly. For emphasis, I nudged Hugo a bit into his side.

"But there's no point in being unreasonable. I like to think I'm a reasonable man. Do you think so?"

A glimmer of hope began gnawing at the fear. The next nod was a little firmer.

"Good! Then there's room for communication, yes?"

The next nod was longer in coming. He had a boss to worry about, one I was sure would resent the man telling tales out of school. But I was, by far, the more immediate concern. The nod came slowly.

I studied his face, especially the eyes, trying to measure the man's spirit. The eyes were good enough to recognize, but they were not the flinty eyes of a killer. The man was a spotter only. He could be manipulated and broken. He was not a pro.

"All right, buddy. We're going to walk, slowly and calmly, out of here. We'll find a taxi and take a little drive, okay?"

The nod was quite adamant and encouraging.

My return warning was equally adamant but far from encouraging. "If at any time along the way I get even the slightest hint you may be considering something foolish, I'll carve you up like a holiday dinner."

His eyes clamped shut as Hugo bit into his ribs. His nod was ferocious.

"Move!" I barked, then thrust him out toward the main terminal. I grabbed up the plastic-wrapped remains of the good Father and followed. We were only ten steps into the busy terminal when the man chose to ignore my warning. He leaped to his right and ran through the building screaming, "Murder! Murder!"

The option was there to drop him, but the population of the large room, plus the presence of two nearby security types, dissuaded me.

I hate encountering amateurs. A pro can be counted on, psyched, challenged, anticipated. But an amateur frequently beats you only because he does the unexpected. The man's flight was one of panic, not calculation. I had pushed him a bit too far, and now I would have to deal with the response.

The alternative I felt best was to go with the sudden change of fortunes, not against them. I turned and ran to the nearest security man, my own voice matching the spotter's in fear and panic. I screamed at the dazed guard about the two bodies in the toilet, and watched with satisfaction as he hailed his comrade-in-arms and bolted for the men's room.

I immediately raced out to the front of the terminal and piled into the first taxi I could see. I directed the startled driver to my hotel and gave the rear window a quick check as we sped off.

There were no troops in pursuit, but then I didn't really expect any. My spotter didn't want to face the law any more than I did. The shout and run had been pure panic, and panic would keep him running, running right back to the source of the whole ordeal.

That is when I would find him again—he and the man who put him up to it. He was running for his life, and Mark 8:35 was very clear on that score.

*For whoever wishes to save his life shall lose it.*

# FIVE

The taxi turned off the Avenida da Liberdade, past Parque Mayer, the small arcade of movie houses and theaters, and drifted the half a block up to the entrance to the Hotel Lisboa Plaza. Harcourt and I had chosen it for its central location and its four-star rating. Theo and his assassin would give most of their attention to the very best, or the very worst, in trying to track me down. It was our belief that by staying in the upper ranges we could escape detection.

I paid the cabbie off and ignored the stunned expression on the doorman's face as he stared at the plastic garbage bag. I approached the main desk, doing my damnedest to convince all and sundry that I belonged.

"Excuse me," I said in English, "I'm looking for friends. Have the Malcolms checked in yet?"

The desk clerk gave a quick appraisal of my beard and tailoring, and turned hesitantly toward the pigeonholes behind him. His hand reached toward the box designated 509 and removed a slip of paper from within.

"Senhor Harcourt?" he asked.

"The same," I responded.

I accepted his reluctant instructions to go directly up. Now both he and the doorman were staring at my unorthodox baggage. I couldn't resist it.

"Parachute luggage," I said with a big grin. "The best!" I then strode off toward the elevators.

The first surprise of the afternoon came when the door to room 509 opened. I found myself staring eyeball to eyeball with one of the most gorgeous Amazons I had ever seen. She was every inch of six feet, with flaming red hair and crisp green eyes that had no fear of shooting through you.

For a moment I stood speechless. She reacted by crossing her arms over her pronounced bosom, leaning herself into the doorframe, and hitting me with one of the thickest Australian accents I had ever heard.

"Right you are, lovey. Five-foot-eleven in me stockin' feet. Now what can I do for ya?"

It took another second before I could conquer the awesome power of her presence. "I believe we have a mutual acquaintance. A Mr. Harcourt?"

Dissecting eyes gave me the once-over. "Not by the look of it, m'love. Harcourt likes 'em a trifle more on the clerical side as I hear it."

I emptied the contents of the garbage bag onto the floor as I responded. "As you can see, I am a man of the cloth. As of late, I've been forced into a somewhat more militant stance on churchly issues."

She eyed the clothing, the blood still wet on the good Father's pants. Her eyes finally returned to me, her body refusing to give one inch in the doorway. "Jamie!" she called.

Behind her appeared a head, my second surprise of the afternoon. If she was an Amazon, he was a Goliath. The man answering the call towered over her by a good seven inches, every inch, from what I could see, built out of the sinewy bedrock. His own hair was a duller shade of red, and his eyes were an arresting shade of steel gray.

If possible, he was even more beautiful than the girl.

He studied me a moment, patted the lady on the shoulder, and answered her in measured, English tones. "It's him, sweet. I've seen photos. Give him a welcome, what?"

With that confirmation, the girl's manner, not to mention her accent, altered drastically. "Sorry. Had to be sure, you know." It was a voice a full tone lower than the one that had greeted me, the new accent as measured as the man's.

She bent down, sweeping the clothing from the floor, and ushered me into the room. I sealed the door behind me as she dumped the clothing in a corner. The man commenced the introductions, his hand stabbing out toward me.

"My name's Jamie Lawler. This is my sister Belinda. To the world, we're the Malcolms from Sydney, Australia." The hand that gripped mine was firm and careful, but the feeling it left was that with the slightest cause for doing so, it could crush you in seconds. "Good to meet you, Carter. We've heard nothing but praise for your talents."

I nodded my appreciation from one to the other, still mesmerized by the sheer grandeur of the two.

"Forgive me," I sighed. "I'm used to dealing with agents of a more subdued stature . . . the anonymous types. You two must have a hell of a time blending in with the crowd."

The resultant laughter from both was warm and welcoming.

"You're not exactly the boy next door yourself," Belinda remarked. "Rather a looker, I'd say."

"Why, thank you, luv!" I said, mocking her accent and turning back to Jamie. "Sorry to drag you out of South Africa. I hope I didn't inconvenience anything."

The man shrugged. "Life with the big top. We go

where the Circus sends us. Personally, I'm rather looking forward to working with the famous N3."

"Ditto," Belinda murmured with a low, throaty chuckle.

I looked over at the beautiful redhead and hoped I detected a double entendre in her comment. Then I turned back to Jamie.

"Do I have a room?" I asked.

"Two, actually," he replied, his hands digging into his trousers and removing a key, which he tossed in my direction. "Should anyone get curious, we've supposedly got you right next door. Five-ten it is."

"But for the sake of privacy," Belinda interjected, "we had MI-6 rent the next room on . . . 511. Harcourt told us a bit about your troubles—a touch of hide and go seek . . . with the seeker having to do a bit of hiding himself. Since you're going to have to have connections with the outside, we thought it would be best if you did it from 510. That way, if anyone wants to trace you down, they'll end up at that door, not yours."

Another key found itself into my hands as I praised their efforts. While I thanked them openly, I thanked Harcourt silently. He had sent me his best. When I had finished, Jamie picked up the conversation.

"We wired 510 up good. If anyone knocks, or enters, legally or otherwise—even if there's a call—it will all register in here."

He pointed toward a miniature TV and portable phone unit resting on the bureau top as he continued. "It's all shortwave, mostly. We have only to flip on the telly, and we can watch whoever it is that's made the entry. The telephone took a bit more wiring, but not even the maids will spot it. Room 510 has adjoining doors on each side. If anyone shows, we can have at them from two sides."

I stared once more at the two of them in open admiration. "My compliments to British ingenuity," I said.

Jamie offered a partial bow. "No disrespect to the Circus, but in all honesty, the designs are ours. One of the advantages of a degree in electronics."

Belinda chimed in. "We may be physically bold, but we're sneaky as hell!"

Jamie rose and clapped me on the back. "Might as well give it its first run. Your man in Washington is most anxious to talk to you." He turned to his sister. "Luv?"

She responded by moving to one of the suitcases in the room and withdrawing a small scrambler unit, which she handed to me.

"Let's see how well it works," she said.

"Right," I said, and took leave of the two beautiful giants to contact Hawk.

I stepped into room 510 and confronted, once more, the thoroughness of Harcourt's minions. The room was stocked with clothing, toilet articles, and tourist material—all the props necessary to convince the world the room was actually *ocupado*. Again I praised the two while I made my connections to Washington.

Hawk's voice was a familiar comfort. I gave him a recap of events before getting down to strategy.

"Any word on your end about the auction?" I asked.

Although his response to my progress had been spirited up to now, his voice sounded downcast at the question. "No," he muttered. "There's been no communication as of yet. Personally, I doubt there will be."

"How do you make it?"

I could hear him chewing at the end of his cigar before he answered. "I think Theo's playing it safe. My guess is that he won't be making any offers to any governments per se. I think he's going to handle it strictly through free-lancers."

The Countess's image danced through my mind. "But why? That'll just cut into his take, won't it?"

Hawk gave an ironic snort. "At the prices we're talking about, what's a few million one way or the other? I think he's more concerned with building a cushion than boosting the price. Governments have too big a reach. If he tried dealing with us directly, we could track him and hang him. With a middleman, we're limited to negotiation."

There was a discouraging sigh before the man continued. "He knows our priorities. First and foremost, we need the nuclear information. He's handing the freelancers blue chip goods. Negotiations could become lengthy. By the time we manage to secure the information, his trail would be colder than the proverbial sorcerer's mammary."

I could afford a glimmer of optimism. I knew about the Countess; Hawk did not. "We'll have to do something about that, won't we?"

Although he may have missed the meaning, Hawk tuned in psychically to the direction of my thoughts. "I don't know about *we*, but *you* are going to have to get into that auction somehow. If you can't get in yourself, you're going to have to make damn sure you control someone who is."

It was with some pleasure that I related to Hawk my meeting with the Countess on the plane. I could sense the other end of the line perking up as I explained her seeming willingness to negotiate a deal. By the time I had outlined the approach I would use in detail, Hawk was chuckling.

If I didn't know better, I could swear the voice on the other end of the line was leering. "Well, well," he growled. "The Countess, heh?"

There was another uncharacteristic chuckle before the man seemed to catch himself and descend back into business.

"Get her, Nick," he said. "Deal with her at any price.

Just make damn sure she takes you into that auction with her. Let her handle the bidding and the negotiations; you just concentrate on N-1!"

There was a certainty in his voice that I just couldn't share. "This is the Countess we're talking about, sir. I can't just hand her the business end without at least keeping half an eye out. To put it politely, she's an opportunist. I'm not sure she can be completely trusted, deal or not."

There was another chuckle from the Washington end. "Does she know you're connected with me?"

I thought a moment. "No. No way she could. She knows I'm in intelligence work, but she doesn't know about AXE. She just assumes I'm with the Company."

"Keep it that way," came the clipped reply. "There's no doubt she'll try to play games, but I'll handle it. Tell her you represent your government, tell her you're on your own—I don't care. But once you've sewn up the deal, once you have the details on the auction, report in to me. I'll handle the Countess. You just worry about our little black sheep, am I clear?"

"As crystal," I said. "Now all we have to do is win the bid."

Sobriety returned to the man across the ocean; sobriety and a further note of confidence I could not share. "We'll get it. I can smell it. Theo will hand it to us."

"I wish I could feel as certain as you."

The voice grew reflective. "Bet on it. Theo was never a simple man. He's full of contradictions. He has damaging material, but he doesn't want to hurt me; he has no reason to. In spite of what's happened or how it looks, his loyalties run deep. I think he's as concerned as we are that the material finds its way back to us."

There was a contemplative silence from both of us as Hawk's words settled. I was the one to finally break it. "Why, sir? Why's he doing it? He takes the goods but wants us to get it back. And if you're right, he'll bury higher bids to do it, so it can't just be the money. Why?"

There was another long pause. The voice, when it finally answered, sounded old for the first time since I had known the man.

"I don't know, Nick. I wish I did!"

I let out a long sigh and then shrugged. "Only Theo himself can give us the answer; let's just hope he's in a talkative mood when I finally get to him. I'll report to you as soon as the deal is set up."

"Be persuasive," was the final reply.

I hung up the phone and sat for a moment, trying to digest the import of the whole damnable situation. This was an assignment unlike any other. In most capers, an agent hits the field and he faces something clear-cut, an enemy. Both sides know the game. They accept it. But this time the rules were different.

Theo was father and teacher; he was founder and master; he was part of me.

I faced a whirlpool. Nothing that merely dragged you down. Nothing you could fight cleanly. Instead I faced an eddy of contrasts and personal memories that only dragged me around in circles. At the bottom, only one thing.

Theo, and all his contradictions.

Then jet lag, fatigue, and general weariness of the mind claimed me.

I stretched out on the bed, closed my eyes, and with a will born from years of training, willed my mind and body to relax.

Within a half hour I was alert and in complete control of Carter Incorporated.

In the cracked marble ambience of the bath, I splashed water on my face and returned to normal; sharp, alert, and wary.

Ten minutes later I made my way back to room 509.

Jamie sat in one of the room's chairs, a scotch gripped in his hand. Belinda peered out the window, the distant ramparts of St. George's Castle topping the skyline. Jamie gestured with his glass as he spoke.

"Help yourself. Your brand, I believe."

"MI-6 thinks of everything," I chuckled, moving to the dresser and pouring myself a drink.

"We do try to please," Jamie grinned.

I sat down at the foot of the bed. It was time to brief my able partners. In a short time they had managed to secure my complete trust. I saw no reason to withhold anything from them, and I proceeded to lay out the whole gory picture.

They listened intently, two minds whirring in harmony with my story. By the time I was finished, two fresh drinks were in hand.

"As I see it, we're limited on the auction," Jamie said. "You're working the entry through the Countess. If what you say of your Mr. N1 is true, it would be by invitation only. No point in trying to get in the back door, correct?"

"Right," I said, nodding. "Theo's too careful. Security will be airtight."

Jamie lifted his glass in mock toast. "Your game, that. Have to work the Countess on your own, I'm afraid."

I returned the toast. "To the Countess. Let's just hope she's as interested in recapturing her emotional youth as she is her physical."

"My money goes with you, Mr. Carter," came Belinda's soft voice from the window.

My eyes turned to the woman. Her body was framed in the window with sunlight pouring in behind her. For the first time, I realized how thin the garment she wore was. The sunlight silhouetted her perfect body, and it was a sight impossible to ignore. No amount of scotch seemed capable of stilling the dryness forming in my throat.

Jamie cleared his throat, bringing my attention back to the business at hand. "That leaves only the aftermath," he said. "Once he's made the sale, he'll burrow deep into a hole. As I understand it, you don't want him getting any deeper than six feet."

"Exactly," I replied with a slight smile. "Any ideas?"

He thought for a moment, swirling the ice in his glass. Belinda cut into his reverie gently. "You thinking what I'm thinking?"

He nodded. "I believe so, luv. Good old Einar Krieger, what?"

"Exactly," she replied.

"Care to explain it to me?" I asked.

Jamie sat forward in his chair. "No one is walking into that auction with cash in hand. I can guarantee it. Your man Theo will no doubt have some sort of collection system set up. That means banks—Swiss banks—if your assumption is correct."

"It would be the most logical," I agreed.

"Let's hope so. When Belinda and I first joined MI-6, we handled a lot of their financial affairs—laundered funds and such. We have good contacts in Switzerland, Einar Krieger being the strongest. He's very highly placed in the Hassen Bank, with connections in Liechtenstein. If your N1 gets anywhere near him, we may be able to do some tracing. It's possible we can come up with his location."

"How long will it take to set up?"

"I can start now," he answered. "At least lay the groundwork. Once you have the arrangement particulars on the exchange of goods, we can put him on it. He'll know what to watch for then."

It was my turn to toast. "My compliments again. And

I was convinced the Swiss were inviolate.''

Jamie turned to his sister, a wide grin breaking over his lips. "There are some things no one can refuse," he winked, then turned back to me. "That only leaves us with the assassin. Any help we can offer there?"

I shook my head. "I'm pretty much on my own there, I'm afraid. It'll be up to me to call off the hunt—or terminate it at the source. The only thing you *can* help with is to narrow the search. How strong are your contacts here in Lisbon?"

He shrugged. "Personally, not too good. But we have the complete cooperation of the Lisbon station. They've been notified by Harcourt to aid us at a moment's notice."

"Good," I nodded. "Have them start tracking down a Julio Martinez. He looks local, but he's Spanish. He won't be using his own name, but he shouldn't be too hard to find. He's not a pro. I'll bet he's left a trail somewhere."

"What's his connection with the affair?" Belinda asked.

"He's the drunk who spotted me at the airport. At the moment, he's sporting three broken fingers. That'll probably be the first place to start the hunt. He'll have to go to someone to get them repaired. Don't count on it being a reputable establishment."

Jamie seemed momentarily confused. "You mean they sent in a spotter you knew?"

"Barely," I replied. "Worked with the man once fifteen years ago. I was on assignment in Madrid. He was an ex-engraver turned paperhanger. I needed some forgery work done, and he pulled it off for me."

"And you remember him?"

I tapped one finger to the side of my head. "Photographic memory," I smiled. "But it took me a while. He's gained thirty pounds, now wears glasses and a mus-

tache, and has lost much of his hair. But it wasn't too difficult to start with the man at the airport and work the
features back in time. I just kept rearranging him, men-
tally, on the taxi ride into town. Finally I came up with
the name."

"Jolly good show!" Jamie grinned. "What do you
want us to do if we find him?"

"Just tail him. Sometime before too long he'll need to
make contact. I want to be there when he does."

"You've got it."

Belinda moved away from the window. "Until then
you'll need rest and fresh clothing," she said, then
chuckled. "You look it and smell it." She moved past
me to the door adjoining our other rooms. Her hand
stretched out to graze my cheek as she passed. "I'll lay
out some things. I hope my taste in clothes meets with
your approval. Short notice and all."

There was an exciting warmth where she had
touched. I watched her disappear into 510, then turned
my attention to her brother. Jamie sat there, his drink
swirling, his face lit by a knowing smile.

"Bit of a minx, what?"

"Look . . ." I started, but his hand came up to still
me.

"No need to explain. It's between you and Belinda to
work out. You, of all people, should know. Sex is one of
the tools of the game. And a very effective tool at that!"
He stood to his full height and raised his glass in my direction. "To success." He grinned broadly.

"And longevity," I quipped.

His rumbling laughter filled the room as he set the
glass down on the desk, clamped me on the shoulder,
and moved to the front door. "Things to do, old boy.
Stiff upper lip . . . or whatever!"

With that, he was gone. I sat and finished my drink,
waiting for Belinda to return to the room. When she

didn't, I retired my glass to the desk and moved through 510 to 511.

The first sight that greeted me was an outfit draped over a chair. I assumed it to be my change of clothes. It was a tasteful ensemble with sweater, slacks, and sport coat, all thoroughly laundered to remove any hint of newness.

The second sight was a little more unsettling. I looked to my left and found Belinda. What had been silhouetted by the sunshine streaming through the window was now displayed in all its considerable glory. Her clothes occupied the room's other chair, and her body occupied the bed.

"I thought you said I needed rest," I said, staring in obvious admiration at the luscious form sprawled before me.

Her brow knitted a moment in concentration. Then she jerked up, her pendulous breasts slapping together as she did. "Of course!" she cried. "How silly of me."

She rose from the bed and approached me. Her hands reached out and undid the belt at my waist. With hardly a second wasted, my pants found their way to the floor. She then circled me with her arms, her lips planting themselves on mine, her tongue exploring my mouth teasingly.

She broke the embrace and smiled up at me. "Forgive the oversight. I'll draw us a bath."

With that she stepped off to the bathroom, her attitude leaving no doubt that she was not coming out. I pulled off my borrowed sweater, stepped out of the slacks, kicked off my shoes and socks, and followed her to enjoy the postures and pleasures of the bath.

# SIX

I lit a cigarette and leaned against the warehouse corner. The docks lay before me, a slight chill biting the midnight air. Beyond lay the Tagus River, the life's blood of Lisbon. It traveled by, a huge, dark swatch, separating me from the southern section of city glittering across the way. My eyes turned right, following the framing lights of the April 25 Bridge over the water.

On the other side stood the huge, floodlit statue of *Cristo-Rei*, Christ the King. The monument soared 110 meters into the air and stood like a concrete exclamation point at the bridge's termination. To most it represented ascending piety; to me it was only another grim reminder of my mission. Like the man I was seeking, it was little more than a mass of contradictions.

Christ, the Shepherd King. Theo, the shepherd priest.

A shudder twisted at my spine, and I turned my back on the view. Theo would consume me enough. For now there was the small matter of my assassin. I drifted down the warehouse wall, putting as much distance as I could between myself and omens of the future. It was time to concentrate on Julio Martinez and who it was that had hired him.

Once more I thanked the ineptness of the man Theo had chosen. Martinez had, indeed, left a trail.

MI-6 had started at the airport. It wasn't difficult to find the cabbie who had driven Julio into Lisbon. A man in pain is hard to forget, especially when a hospital is not the destination. Once the area where Martinez had been dropped could be pinpointed, MI-6 moved into high gear.

Cashing in on an Anglo-Portuguese cooperation that extends back to 1371, British Intelligence called in the locals. The area known, it wasn't difficult to locate the doctor—an underground regular. Although addresses had never been exchanged, Martinez had been forced to drop a name or two in order to enlist the physician's aid, names no doubt from his own past, not his employer's.

One of the beauties of the underworld lowlife is its unimaginativeness. Names reveal networks. The doctor knew the references well, and since house calls were frequently required of him, he was able to offer a small list of hotels most often utilized by the quoted parties.

The various stakeouts were quickly arranged—and just as quickly rewarded. Martinez was spotted, his bandaged hand glowing like a calling card, heading for an outside phone booth. For him, the first call was unanswered; for us, it was a gold mine. The Portuguese authorities were politely thanked and then dismissed as MI-6 set up to run the show.

Martinez's room was located, the building was covered, and the outside booth wired to the hilt. There were two more phone attempts before paydirt was struck. Martinez reached his party around six o'clock, and a midnight meet was arranged, all duly recorded by British electronics.

The site was then examined, a seedy dockworkers' bar called *Cidade Rio*, River City. Appropriate costuming was provided, and all that remained now was for Jamie to come and announce the arrival of our pigeon.

The bird, broken wing or not, was prompt. A match flared at the end of the street. Jamie was calling me. I moved quickly and quietly toward him, my cigarette crushed into blackness at his feet.

"He just went in," the giant man said, gesturing back down the narrow side alley. "So far, it would appear he's the first to arrive."

"Good," I said, adjusting the bulk of my fisherman's sweater to better hide the gun at my side and the knife strapped to my arm. "Think I'll pass?"

Jamie stared at me appraisingly. "The makeup's good—can't tell you from the scum inside." He chuckled. "The hair's a bit too straight, though. You might do better with this."

He pulled the knit cap from his own head and set it onto mine. I adjusted it quickly as Jamie spelled out the arrangements.

"We've got three men watching all the ins and outs. Couldn't afford to crowd the place up now, could we? There's also a car, about two blocks off, that can be here in seconds. All you have to do is hit this, and you'll have men and machines coming at you like William at Hastings."

He handed me a pack of local cigarettes and a miniature electronic sender shaped like an ancient Zippo lighter.

"Just lay them on the table next to you. Light the lighter, and we're on our way. Should anything out here catch our attention, we'll let you know by sending a signal of our own. It'll register on this. You'll feel a small but definite jolt of electricity."

He slipped a small ring onto my finger. "Congratulations! We've just become engaged."

"I'm honored," I retorted. "I'm also impressed. I take it I have you to thank for the craftsmanship?"

His nod was a modest, gentle affirmation.

"How many inside?" I asked.

"Five. Hard-core locals all. They shouldn't give you a bother, I'd say. From what I understand, if they do, the odds are about even."

I smiled at the compliment. "You know that, and I know that. Maybe they haven't read the notices."

"It'll be their undoing then, won't it?" he said with a grin, then grew sober. "I think it's time you went in. Company should be arriving shortly. Good luck, Carter."

I slapped the man on his shoulder and moved off toward the tavern lights.

I entered a room thick with smoke and the smell of sardines. Three men occupied a scarred wooden bar to my right, while two more stared at me from a table to my left. My eyes ignored them all, traveling to the very back of the small room.

Martinez sat in the farthest booth, his back to me, his bandaged hand resting gingerly on the table. The pale light of the room lit the side of his face, catching glimmering beads of sweat as they rolled down his brow. Whatever fear I had given him at the airport seemed undiminished by the ensuing hours.

His ordeal was just beginning.

I moved quickly to the table, arranging myself in a chair across from him. It took a second for his artist's eyes to pierce the thin disguise, but once they did, they bugged to frightening proportions. His body jerked toward flight, but my quick grasp of his injured hand halted the movement.

"Don't!" was all I barked, but the cold command in

my whispered voice seemed to cripple the muscles in his body. Just to be sure, I popped Hugo into my palm beneath the table.

He stared a full minute before words could make their way past the lump in his throat. The voice was frail but committed as it returned in whispered threat. "I'll scream. I swear I will. I'll scream my lungs out."

My body indicated surrender, but my mind framed the attack. While I released his hand, my eyes scanned the room. The five men were glancing cautiously toward the two strangers in the back, but none seemed any more than just curious. The odds were in my favor.

"You don't want to do that," I warned, but Martinez was adamant.

"Touch me again, and I will."

My left hand rose up. "No touch, no scream. Deal?"

There was a weak responding nod, but the lie was written in the rapid darting of his eyes. Within a heartbeat, the move followed. He got no farther than the breath it takes to bolt, before Hugo lifted from under the table, drove into his injured hand, and embedded itself an inch and a half into the tabletop.

The scream that followed was one of agony, not fear.

My eyes shifted to study the bar's occupants. All five stared in rapt curiosity. I glared back, greeting each pair of eyes with a look that spelled death. Gradually, one by one, the eyes of the strangers flickered away, leaving Martinez to his fate.

My attention returned to the Spaniard. He sat slumped in his chair, tears of pain squeezing from the corners of his eyes.

"I hate liars," I hissed in Spanish. "I never touched you, and yet you screamed. If you start out lying, how can I possibly believe anything else you're about to tell me?"

The man stared at the blade rising out of his palm, his face a blanket of sweat. "What do you want of me?" he gasped.

"You're meeting someone. Who is it?"

His head swiveled violently from side to side. "I don't know."

Before the man could even blink, Hugo lifted and fell a second time, entering the palm just behind the thumb. A fresh rivulet of blood burst forth as the man again screamed, swooned to his left, and vomited on the floor.

I allowed the spasm to pass before continuing. "Someone out there is trying to kill me, my friend. I get impatient when I'm hunted. You're a talented artist, Martinez, but you're going to be a starving one if you don't start answering questions. So far I've been gentle, but next time I start severing the tendons, one by one. How well will you be forging with a useless hand?"

The understanding he nodded was that of a shattered man. The voice was barely audible as he spoke. "What do you wish to know?"

"Who hired you?"

The face lifted, a study in fear and anticipation. "I swear it! I do not know." I flexed my fingers over Hugo's hilt, but the voice cut in quickly. "It was dark! A room in Madrid. There were lights in my face. I heard only the man's voice. I never saw him. He gave me an envelope of drawings—pictures of you in various disguises. I was told to study them, make my own arrangements, and station myself at the airport."

"What about the other two men that were with you?"

"Mine . . . I hired them. I was given money to do this. Money and a telephone number to which I would report afterward. That is all I know!"

The man was too far gone to be lying. His words only confirmed my suspicions. So far, the whole setup reeked

of Theo's brainwork. But that was Theo; the *killer* had
to have made mistakes.

"Who answered when you called the number? Why
are you meeting here?"

"I do not know such things. A voice. I spoke with a
voice I've never heard. I was told to come here, so I
came. I do not know why. Another attempt, perhaps.
That is all I know."

"Why come at all?" I pursued. "Why not run, Julio?
You did your job. You failed, but you were through.
Why did you come?"

I would have thought it impossible, but the man's eyes
showed an even greater depth of fear, his tone a mirror
of those emotions. "The voice, *señor*. One does not ignore that voice. It is the voice of death."

The British recording of the earlier call ran through
my brain. There was nothing in it to justify the terror I
was witnessing. "You mean the man on the phone?" I
asked.

His head shook. "The room, *señor*. The man behind
the lights. A voice that steals your will." With a greater
fear to occupy his emotions, his response to me became
one of hatred. "It is a voice I pray you meet. He will kill
you, and I will piss on your grave."

There was a haunting quality to the comment, one I
could not allow to linger. I pulled the knife from his
hand and stabbed it into the tabletop to my right. My
hands freed, I laid Jamie's gift of cigarettes and lighter
onto the table.

"I look forward to it, my friend. That I promise you.
Will this mysterious voice be joining you this evening?"

"Perhaps yes, perhaps no. We shall soon see," he
answered.

I smiled in the glare of his spite. "If not, it will be
someone one step closer. I'll find him, Martinez. In the

meantime, we'll just have to wait. A drink might be nice to pass the time."

I turned toward the bar, my hand preparing to order, when the first jolt of doubt gripped my stomach. There was no one behind the bar. For that matter, there had not been anyone there since I had walked in.

It's the little things that'll kill you.

It's one thing for the bartender to make a quiet and occasional retreat—the stockroom, the bathroom—all easily overlooked during the occasional checks by MI-6. It's another for him to disappear entirely. My eyes made a quick scan of the five occupants. They were sipping, not drinking, which meant they knew the service would be slow.

Rugged, thirsty fisherman don't sip. They gulp.

The room suddenly reeked of setup.

At that moment the ring provided by Jamie came to life. I felt the subtle burst of a current pecking at my finger. Company was on its way. My gaze lifted toward the door, but my intent was as much to lock the room into my peripheral vision as it was to greet our approaching guest. Even as my right hand crawled beneath my sweater toward Wilhelmina, the setup began crystalizing in my mind.

Theo keeps handing me over, and the assassin keeps bungling the opportunities. Sooner or later Theo is going to cash in on it. Both of us were pro enough to spot the trend. Once established, Theo had only to start maneuvering his inept help like morsels of cheese, and yours truly would find himself finessed right into the middle of the trap.

My eyes darted back to Martinez. He was staring at me, his expression one of anticipation, not betrayal. He was awaiting his voice. I was preparing for Armageddon. I felt a twinge of pity for the forger. Twenty-five or so years in the business, and the man had not yet learned that the cheese is expendable.

I quickly scanned the room. To my right was a faded blue curtain, a remnant from the days when this bar had pretensions to class. It was split down the center, its tattered edges revealing a wooden backing. Behind the backing was the narrow hall that led to the bathroom.

I deposited Wilhelmina in my lap and returned my focus to the door. As I did, I brought both of my hands onto the table and removed a cigarette from the pack. I placed it in my mouth and tilted myself back onto the rear legs of my chair. I twirled the cigarette in my mouth a moment, waiting until I heard the approach of footsteps before reaching for the lighter.

I riveted my eyes back on the doorway, but my concentration was anywhere but. The man about to enter was a sham. There was no meeting. All that would come through that door was another spotter, a pair of eyes instructed to pierce the gloom, seek me out, and assure my identity to the five men in the room. Once assured, they would see me erased like graffiti from an altar.

I allowed my peripheral sight to analyze the situation. The man at the end of the bar and the two at the table were facing me, their hands in plain view. The other two at the bar were hunched forward, their backs a perfect shield. When trouble came, it would be from that quarter first.

A body framed itself in the doorway, paused a second, and stepped in. I brought the lighter up to my cigarette, cupping it in both hands, making sure I obscured my face in the process. I studied the man trying so desperately to study me. It was no one I knew, but then it didn't figure to be. It's one thing to pick one face out of hundreds at an airport. That calls for previous experience.

There was only one face for this man to look at: mine. Photographs would do just fine. The man struggled to recreate the various pictures as he scanned my face, but I kept my hands cupped around the cigarette, blocking his view.

Then I saw no reason to delay the inevitable.

I flicked the lighter to life, lowering my left hand as I did so. My hope was for two things. First, that I was sending my signal; I wanted Jamie and his friends to know the shit was nearing the fan. And second, I wanted the patsy in the doorway to see what he needed. He saw his fill.

With the light to help him pierce the darkness, identification was instantaneous. His eyes sparkled with recognition, so much so that he failed to notice me setting the unextinguished lighter beneath the curtain to my right. No sooner had I done so then my hand jumped down to my lap and the comforting feel of Wilhelmina.

With recognition came action. As the man opened his mouth to confirm my existence, I thrust my chair backward, rolling onto the floor. My final act before doing so was to remove the left side of his face.

What the man was no longer capable of doing, I had done myself. With the first bark of gunfire, the men at the bar moved swiftly. Both swiveled on their stools and leveled two sawed-off shotguns at the booth. The twin blasts were deadly and deafening.

I was barely aware of Martinez's eerie cry as I returned the favor. Two quick belches from Wilhelmina, and the shotguns—and their owners—clattered to the floor. I gave a quick glance to the end of the bar, but the man there had already found cover. That left only the man at the table.

Unfortunately for me, both were very quick in responding. Both had managed to produce pistols, and both began firing before I could really get a bead on them. But fortunately for me, Martinez chose that moment to drop to the floor. Two of the bullets shredded the wood of the floor near my face, but the other three implanted themselves in the lifeless hulk of the forger.

I took the opportunity to retreat backward behind the cover of the wooden hall and the sheet of fire that was now spreading out from my booth. Three more shots pierced the air, but all they yielded were fragments of wood as they tore through the burning partition above me.

Then came silence.

The fire was doing its job. Without it, the three men remaining could have gotten around the partition from any number of directions. With it, there was only one way to reach me—dead-on in my firing line—and Wilhelmina was ready for just such an approach.

There was one other option, and I was hoping they would see it. They could wait. They knew one thing. The fire was growing, and I was no more impervious to its effects than they. Sooner or later I would have to escape it myself. It would reach me before it reached them, and all they had to do was nail me when I bolted.

What I hoped they couldn't know was that the same lighter that had started the conflagration was also busy summoning aid. I waited for the first sounds of new gunfire before committing myself. MI-6 arrived, and just in time.

The first sounds of secondary battle rang through the tiny room just as the burning remnants of my tablecloth hit the floor in front of me. The two men at the table had obviously moved over to the bar. I could hear the explosions of gunfire and glass as the window behind them burst into fragments.

At the same time, the fifth man who had previously

occupied the end of the bar suddenly appeared before me. His head peered out from my end of the counter, his eyes intent on the door that led to the back room. While his eyes tasted salvation, the rest of him perished. Wilhelmina barked once more, drilling him straight through the temple.

I waited a second longer as the battle waned, relieved to hear Jamie's familiar voice.

"Carter! Are you there?"

"Yeah," I answered. "I'm coming out. Get the car in front, and keep your face down!"

Even as I spoke, I lifted myself up and turned the corner on the flaming booth. I reached Jamie, tearing the hat from my head and slapping it into his hands. "Put this on—quick! Pull it down over your eyes, and get the hell into that car as fast as you can."

There was a screeching of tires in front of the bar, and the two of us moved quickly toward it. The car door flew open, and we piled in. Even as we moved, gunfire burst from the rooftops above us. Two of Jamie's allies dropped like cement.

"Move it!" I yelled to the driver, and the man complied with a raucous squeal of tires. The next few seconds were lost as Jamie and I rolled around the back seat, but once clear of the ambush site, sanity returned with a quick, barked command from me. The driver settled down to a pace that would enable us to maintain our seats.

"What the hell was that all about?" Jamie panted.

"A goddamned setup," I growled.

Jamie blinked. "Setup? How could it be? We trailed the son-of-a—"

"We were supposed to," I interjected. "Theo's finally figured out who he's working with. He knew I'd track Martinez down. He was counting on it."

Jamie tore off the cap and used it to wipe the sweat from his brow. "My, my," he said, then chuckled. "Your boy doesn't miss a trick, does he?"

"Not too often," I replied as the cap found its way into my own hands.

Jamie's chuckle worked its way into a laugh. "Well, he failed this time, what? He missed you this go-round!"

I studied the man before answering. "Yeah, he missed me. But he got something else. I'll bet on it."

"What's that?"

I stared out the window. "He knows I need cover. AXE is blown, so that eliminates normal channels. I'd have to go somewhere else for help."

Jamie nodded. "Of course. You came to us. So what? He could assume MI-6 would be your first choice."

I kept searching the passing doorways as though Theo himself might suddenly appear. "He can assume, but he doesn't know for sure, right?"

"Right!"

When I turned to face the man, he must have sensed my concern. His smile faded, and my words seemed to hit him like mallets. "You remember the gunshots as we left the bar?"

His own look grew grave. "I have two men back there on the pavement, and you can ask a question like that?"

"I know, Jamie, and I'm sorry. But there are *two* things in this business that someone can shoot you with, and both are deadly. One is bullets . . . the other is *film*."

Slowly the realization spread across Jamie's face. "My God . . ."

"Exactly," I said, then turned to once again stare out the window at the bleak darkness. "He may have missed me, my friend, but I'm scared to death that he got you."

# SEVEN

The Ritz was every inch the deluxe hotel its name would imply. Built in the fifties, it was given the worldwide exposure in a *Life* magazine article that made its name synonymous with luxury. I could picture the Countess in no other setting.

But I was not here to sightsee.

I made a quick trip through the marbled lobby and up the ornately paneled elevator. I checked my watch and stepped up to the door of the Countess's suite.

The lady appreciated promptness, and I would give it to her down to the second. One o'clock registered itself on the face of my AXE-issue watch, and I knocked.

Almost instantly the door slid open to reveal the pampered face of Gustav. He was dressed in conservative pinstripes, his thinning hair combed over his skull to hide the baldness so evident in spite of his efforts. He took a moment to study my face.

"Mr. Carter," I offered. "I have an appointment."

He merely nodded and stepped back. I walked past him, the pungent odor of perfume assailing my nostrils. It wasn't until he had closed the door and bade me follow that I realized the scent was his. Whatever pleasures her newly reclaimed youth offered, the Countess obviously didn't extend them to her associates.

He minced his way down a narrow hall and ushered me into the suite's large sitting room. He motioned me to sit, clicked his heels, and coasted out through one of the room's two doors. My eyes followed his progress and then flickered around to absorb the grandeur of the surroundings.

Thick white carpeting coated the floors, and rising up from it was a collection of antique furniture that might have been lifted from any museum in Europe. Everything—from the Turner landscapes on the wall to the satin curtains that framed the terrace—spoke of wealth and luxury.

I wandered over to the terrace doors and enjoyed the view. The Countess's room looked out over Edward VII Park. Below me were the *crème de la crème* of the European crop, walking their poodles and laughing off last night's losses at the Estoril Casino. I envied them the simplicity of their decadence.

My own adventures of the previous night had left me somewhat shaken. It was one thing to accept Martinez's death and the dead-end it implied. It was quite another to feel I had been outpsyched.

Where the assassin was concerned, I had worked out my keys. *Follow the execution, not the planning!* And the keys had worked. They had gotten me through the attempt at the airport, and they had found me Martinez himself. That Theo would eventually pick up on this and use it was inevitable. It was even desirable.

There are certain dynamics to any caper. An agent starts out by facing an enemy whose motives and methods are basically unknown. There are two ways to go at him. An agent can either play a waiting game, watching his quarry, noting the trends, studying the opposition until he finds a way to outflank him. Or he can go straight at him, putting himself in the enemy's way, pushing all the buttons until he finds the ones that will generate a response.

Where Theo was concerned, time and circumstance demanded the latter approach.

The danger in this method was that the agent becomes highly visible. He makes himself a target. But that's what he's trained to handle. If he can survive the assaults, he will gain the subtle advantage of control. The minute the enemy begins anticipating your moves, you know what he is thinking. You can begin manipulating events to your own advantage. You start feeding the opposition until he's sure he has you. Then you pull the rabbit out of the hat and nail him.

All very basic: Agentry 101. And who taught me those lessons?

Theo!

It was this fact that was beginning to generate the haunting doubt that maybe the keys had never been. Within me was the unshakable feeling that I was being run—controlled—by the master himself.

Because of Theo's defection, AXE channels were closed to me. Help would have to be sought elsewhere, and he knew it. A good agent would feed me clues, drawing me in until both myself and my cover were exposed. But a good agent might also get anxious and reveal his strategy too soon.

A master would feed me hints and let me work it out for myself.

It was my fear that Theo had done just that. And if he had—if there were more than guns on the rooftops across from that bar last night—I could thank myself for committing a cardinal error. I had exposed Jamie and Belinda.

The three of us had later considered this possibility, and it is to their credit that they were easier on me than I was on myself. They were used to being visible; their size necessitated it. It was finally decided that they would remain at the Plaza, wire their room just as they had wired mine, bunk in with me, and wait to see who turned up.

We no longer had *secrecy*, but we still had *sneaky as hell*.

"Lesson number one, dear boy, never look pensive. It lets the opposition know you're worried."

The voice startled me from my reveries as it bubbled across the room. I did my best to erase both thoughts and accompanying expression as I turned to greet my hostess. Although words tried to form in my mind, they dissipated at the sight that greeted me.

The Countess stood grandly in the doorway, her blouse a billowing white sheath of layered chiffon that allowed the barest hint of nipple to be seen, her skirt a vibrant, red splash of moiré silk. Again my expression must have mirrored my thoughts.

"Better," she purred. "Still not up to business standards, but very flattering. Can I fix you a drink? Scotch, I believe?"

"Two fingers. Neat."

I studied her admiringly as she floated over to the drink cabinet. There was an aura of sensuality to the lady that defied definition. It wasn't a question of communicating maturity. Plastic surgery had eliminated the unwanted years; what remained was a bold statement of experience.

She poured and moved toward me, my drink extended in outstretched elegance.

"I trust you found your way through customs without too much difficulty?" she smiled.

"You have my thanks," I said, executing a slight bow.

"My entry was not as entertaining as yours, but quite simple nonetheless." My gratitude was genuine. The Countess would never know just how much grief her act of charity had saved me.

"Good. Shall we sit?"

She moved over to the sofa and eased into the plush cushions, curling her legs girlishly beneath her. I joined her, my eyes once again admiring the miraculous transformation. She caught my stare and laughed lightly.

"Give it time, dear boy. You'll forget."

"Forget what?"

"Come, come, Nick, there's no need to be coy," she chided. "Cosmetic surgery is the true miracle of our age. A flick of the knife and years fall away. But what the surgeon cannot remove is the memory of others. You see me now, but somewhere in your mind is another image, a mental photograph of what I was. That memory will keep superimposing itself, but in time it will blur and vanish."

"What made you decide to do it?" I asked, taking a sip of my drink and leaning back on the sofa.

The look that passed over her face was uncharacteristically vulnerable. She took a sip of her own drink before answering. "Did you know that Ivan passed away?" she said finally.

"No, I didn't. I'm sorry."

"It was all very quick and painless, really. A heart attack. Even in death he was submissive and obedient. The surprise to me was that I suddenly found I missed the creature."

There was a warmth in her words that brought a smile to my face. For whatever reason, the dynamo that was Irena Voslovich was opening herself to more human emotions. I was glad to discover that more than just the face had changed.

"Not that I could ever be called the model wife, you

understand," she continued. "I've certainly had my share of liaisons. But Ivan did engender a kind of loyalty. He was my creation, in a way, and I felt a responsibility for him."

"He was a kind man," I added.

"Yes, he was," she said. "Very kind. He was a shaggy little puppy who would sit up and do tricks when ordered. But he *loved*, Nicholas. A kind of simple, giving love that people like you and me will never be capable of. And when he died, I suddenly felt the absence of that love."

"Did you think the surgery would help?" I asked gently.

She eyed me sharply, then a low chuckle bubbled from her throat. "The fate of the mature woman is one you will never realize, Nicholas. While men grow *distinguished*, women become *well preserved*. It rather makes one feel like marmalade. I took a hard look at what I could expect out of my canned femininity and didn't like the prospects. I stared at a profusion of doddering, useless old men, or firebrand gigolos, and felt like screaming!"

"Lots of attention but no sincerity?"

"Exactly!" she chimed, her glass saluting me. "So, I sought a third alternative. Youth, even manufactured youth, is rife with advantages. If I'm going to be *preserved*, let me be brought out for picnics—to hell with the catered affairs!" She laughed in delight at her own words.

My own glass lifted in toast. "To Ivan. I never knew he had it in him."

Her glass dropped teasingly. "Don't be tacky, Nicholas. If the sneaky little son-of-a-bitch were alive today, I'd kill him."

"To youth, then . . . youth and picnics."

"Amen!" she said enthusiastically, and drained her glass. "Another?" she asked.

"Wouldn't mind a drop or two."

She relieved me of my glass and moved off to the bar for refills.

"But enough of tawdry melancholy. I have a sudden thirst for the butchery of the marketplace. Talk to me, Nicholas. Make me an offer I can damn well refuse!"

It took a second to slip into business gear, but once I had, I opted for a direct approach. "As I understand it, there is going to be an auction very soon."

She answered as she poured. "Tomorrow, to be exact. The assembly is to gather at St. George's Castle at five o'clock."

The ease with which she offered the information momentarily shocked me. "Are you aware of what exactly is being sold?"

"As I understand it, some of your fellow countrymen have been a bit careless with their papers."

"I suppose you could say that. At any rate, it's an error we want corrected as quickly as possible."

She turned from the bar and eyed me sharply. *"We?"*

"I represent my government."

"And what can your government offer me that another government cannot?" she asked, moving back to the sofa and handing me my drink.

"We can offer you a blank check and the privilege of naming your own price."

"So can the Russians," she said with a shrug.

I paused to think. I felt as if I were spinning wheels. She was right, of course; there was little I could offer that could not be matched elsewhere. As I sipped my scotch I recalled Hawk's conversation regarding Theo's contradictory nature. I wasn't as convinced as the Old Man that Theo wanted us to get the goods back, but it was the only slim hope I could offer.

"Maybe they can," I said. "But I can give you one thing they can't. If you line up with us, I can promise you you'll come away with the prize."

A sharply raised eyebrow greeted my words. "You can guarantee it? How?"

"The man who lifted the goods was an intimate. The motive was money, not politics. He didn't hesitate to burn us, but he doesn't necessarily want us incinerated. It's our belief that he's as interested as we are that the goods return home. Once he knows you're dealing with us, he'll make damn sure you win."

Her eyes bored into me, measuring the commitment and reasoning behind my words. "If what you say is true, we might have a deal. It could well give me the edge I need. But just how are we to let this man know I'm on the side of the angels?"

I grinned. "That's where you earn your commission. You'll have to get me into the auction with you."

There was no hesitation in her response. "Impossible! The ground rules were very clear and very definite. We are to participate *alone*."

"That's the price tag." I shrugged. "Get me in, and I promise you the goods are yours."

"And if I try to accommodate you and find myself disqualified in the process, I gain nothing. Without you I can at least negotiate."

"With me you'll win, and you'll do so without having to invest your own capital."

She rose from the sofa and strode over to the terrace doors. Her focus drifted from the glass in her hand to the view over the park as she weighed the options. Now was the time to press my point in an attempt to swing the scales.

"I'm not asking you to risk anything, Countess. I'm

only asking you to try. If they shut you down, I'll back out gracefully. I'll compose a letter tonight delegating you as our representative at the negotiations. When it comes time to bid, write out your offer on the letter and submit it. The man will recognize the coding and the handwriting. It should do the trick."

She turned from the terrace to face me. "You're clever, dear boy. I've never seen you bow out of anything . . . gracefully or no."

I acknowledged the observation. "True. Countess. But this time I have no choice. The man running the show is too good. There won't be any cracks to crawl through. I either walk in the front door or not at all."

Once more her eyes dissected me. "And you want in very badly, don't you? You're not contemplating anything rash, I hope?"

I returned the gaze. "How do you mean?"

"The man cannot be too popular at home."

I smiled. "Nothing rash, I promise you. Not until the goods find their way home, at any rate."

There was another prolonged study before the Countess swung away from the window, deposited her drink on the end table, and stood next to me, her hand extended.

"I think we have a deal, Nicholas. There will be a substantial agent's fee—payable in advance—in case your assumptions on the auctioneer's intentions prove false. Beyond that, there will be an even more substantial fee for my services as your government's representative and for handling the subsequent transaction itself. Are we in agreement?"

"A fair enough bargain," I said, nodding. I reached for the extended hand.

"Good. I'll have Gustav draw up the papers immediately. I would appreciate it if you could contact your own people and initiate the transfer on the advance. Should events proceed as you envision them, the advance can be deducted from the final fee. You may use the phones here. I assure you they are quite safe. I shall return shortly."

With that, she disappeared through a far door.

I contemplated calling Hawk directly but opted against it. Although she had guaranteed the safety of her phones, safety was a relative reality at best. Safe from outsiders did not promise me that *she* was not recording events. I didn't want Hawk's voice heard by anyone—that was SOP. Instead I phoned Jamie and gave him the appropriate data for forwarding. By the time the call had concluded, the Countess was back.

She approached me and handed over a sheaf of papers. I read through them quickly, satisfied with all but one point.

"There's no mention here of getting me in."

There was a cutting slyness in her smile. "That contract represents our deal in regard to the auctioned material. I consider that to be business. Getting you in I consider to be an unnecessary risk—and a favor. That comes with a different price tag."

Anger flushed my face as I stared into her eyes. "Countess, we had a deal . . ."

"Hush, dear Nicholas," she purred, plucking the papers from my hand and dropping them onto the end table. "These can be dealt with later. Favors demand favors, and they are usually negotiated in more . . . intimate surroundings."

She took my hands and raised me from the couch. Her arms drifted up and circled my neck as her body stepped in to press warmly against me. Her chin lifted, and I tasted the sweetness of her lips as they settled onto mine.

The kiss was warm, sensual, and lingering. When at last it ended, I smiled down at her. "Countess, I think we may have just reached a meeting of the minds."

"Good," she smiled. "Let us see what else we can bring together."

She stepped back and held my hand, slowly guiding me toward the room's second door.

We entered her bedroom, a room no less sumptuous than the one we had departed. It, too, was a study in antique luxury, but the center of focus was the huge mahogany bed with its canopy of fringed swag.

The Countess deposited me on the nearest side, and she traveled around to the other. Quietly she removed the clothing from her body, tossing the blouse and skirt onto a chair. There was nothing else to remove. By the time I was able to join her in nakedness, she was already stretched across the satin bedcover.

She watched me struggle with my clothes, her eyes misty beneath long black lashes, her dark nipples alive, her white skin aglow, her mouth curved in a sensuous smile.

She was playing the role of the whore to the hilt, testing my interest in her, baiting me as I approached the bed.

"Come, Nicholas," she whispered. "Let us seal our contract."

My lips descended on hers as my body covered her lush nakedness. Moans bubbled from deep in her throat as I let my hands wander freely over her warm, supple flesh. Gently yet insistently, I enfolded the firmness of one ample breast, my hand kneading its pliant softness. I lowered my lips to the nipple and teased it deliberately before shifting to do the same to its twin.

She stirred beneath me, urging my fondling of her smooth thighs and wide, womanly hips as my lips continued to devour first one puckered, aroused nipple and then the other.

"Ohhh, yes, Nicholas," she groaned. "Yessss!" Her hands came up to clutch at my hair and force my mouth down harder on her heaving breasts.

Then I began moving my kisses lower, lower on her body, bringing her to an uncontrollable tremble, causing her to strain every muscle of her thighs as they arched to meet my searching mouth.

Perspiration had formed beads all over her body, and she began to gently curse me in a muttering growl as I explored all the rich hills and valleys of her womanliness. Her hips were undulating wildly now, her fingers like talons in my hair, forcing my mouth harder and deeper into her hungry flesh.

"Nick! Ohh, Nicholas, please . . . please, you're driving me crazy!" she cried.

Reluctantly I left the honeyed sweetness between her thighs and moved back up over her luscious, sweat-slick body. Her eyes were closed, her face a tight mask of passion, her hair in tangled disarray where it fanned over the satin pillow. As I bent to kiss her parted lips, a shuddering tremor raced through her, and a groan seeped from deep in her throat.

"Please . . . please, Nicholas . . . I need you . . . *now*!"

I poised above her for one brief instant, and then I took her with every ounce of masculine strength that was in me, my thighs driving forward, again and again, slapping against her heated flesh.

"Yes!" she screamed. "Oh, God, *yesssss*!"

The frenzied lashings of her insatiable body drove me to an incredible state of desire and passion, and both of us were quickly caught up in the torrent and swept along by the unleashed fury.

I groaned with pleasure as her response became even more vigorous, more engulfing, more demanding. Within seconds I knew I was beyond the point-of-no-return. I could feel the mounting sensation gather in force and fury as she bucked and writhed in wanton abandon beneath me, answering each of my thrusts with powerful, engulfing lunges of her own. Her long, sharp fingernails raked at the bare skin of my back and buttocks, forcing me deeper, deeper into her steaming depths. It was so excruciatingly pleasurable that it bordered on pain. Then I felt as though my insides were being broken into a thousand pieces.

I heard my own triumphant cry mingled with her broken and feverish moans. She pulled at me, tore at me, draining each second of ecstasy for all she could get. So complete was my delirium of pleasure that I wasn't aware of the heart-straining descent to normality until I felt myself lying apart from her and tasting the blood on my lips and the scraping sting on my back and shoulders.

I rolled to my side and struggled to bring my breathing back to normal. When I looked over to where the Countess lay, her eyes were closed, a satisfied smile twisting her lips.

Then she opened her eyes and looked up at me. "God! If I could, I'd have Dr. Perelli knighted!" she giggled.

I leaned over and planted a wet kiss on the tip of her nose. "Lady," I said, "there are some things not even science can improve on."

# EIGHT

St. George's Castle is considered by Lisboans to be the cradle of their city. Perched high above the harbor, its stone walls and ramparts are a rising conglomeration of the city's varied history, from the roughened stone of its Visigothic foundations, through the walls of Moorish occupation, right up to the crenelated peaks of its Christian liberation. Even its decidedly Anglican name reflects the English/Portuguese cooperation that helped to rid the nation of its hated Saracens.

I stood at the low stone balustrade surrounding the courtyard and stared out over the city. It seethed like a sea of red tiled roofs spilling its way down to the Tagus River. To my left was a small cluster of Japanese tourists, their cameras and voices clattering away, obviously delighted by the spectacle they witnessed.

For me, there was only anticipation . . . and dread.

The anticipation was mental. The moment was nearing when I would face Theo, eye to eye. He was the enemy. I was forcing myself to remember that. The auction would be dealt with, and Hawk's theories would be proven or disproven. That was the work, the stuff I lived with day to day. I was ready, even eager for it to begin.

Beyond that was the gut-level agony of my task, the inner battle that had crept up on me, little by little, ever since I'd learned the name of my enemy.

"Damn you," I muttered, laying my clammy hands on the stone wall, trying, in some way, to steal a little of the solidity and permanence it represented. I had to forget. Forget the teacher, forget the brilliance, forget the friend. I could only allow myself to see the infidel.

Then, suddenly, I realized there was a different perspective to this confrontation.

I would soon be facing Theo, true, but he would be facing me also. Would he be shocked? Scared? Would he suddenly discover the same doubts and agonies I had? I had spent so much time measuring myself against the master that I had lost sight of the fact that *he* would have to measure me also.

And just how did N1 rate N3?

One thing I was sure of. The man could not view me with indifference.

I turned away from the harbor and faced back into the courtyard. The Japanese group had photographed the view from every possible angle and were now marching their way toward the inner castle, lenses snapping happily at the strolling peacocks and flamingos hovering nearby.

Then my gaze settled on the courtyard's other assembly. In the center of the opening was the huge bronze statue of Alfonso Henriques, first king of Portugal. Next to it stood the Countess, her hair piled stylishly atop her head, her body relaxed and erect. Around her ranged four men, each in varying states of anticipation, each ignoring and yet totally absorbed in the others.

Birds of an entirely different feather.

Of the four men, I knew three. To my right, his toe digging idly at the base of a huge cork tree, was

Egerklein. Thin, bony to the point of appearing like a cadaver, he was a West German manufacturer with more than his fair share of East German affiliations.

Welcome the Iron Curtain!

To the left of the statue, his manner as reposed and stoic as the Countess's, stood Kiang. His squat Oriental body was firmly encased in a finely tailored suit. He was an international merchant based out of Hong Kong, and though he claimed a hatred of the Communist forces that drove him out of China, he made far too many clandestine trips back home to convince those in intelligence circles.

Welcome the Bamboo Curtain!

Behind the statue, and pacing with all the pent-up revolutionary fervor that guided his life, was Alibaz. He was small, lithe, and even though nearing forty, still dressed like the college student he was when his missionary zeal was born. His affiliation was with any group that promised terror, but his motives and backing fairly stank of Libyan oil money.

The Third World has arrived!

The group's only stranger to me stood farther off to my left. He was a huge, barrel-chested giant of a black man. He gave one the impression of being a tribal chief, removing himself from the contaminating presence of the hated whites.

Black Africa had found its way into the international espionage market!

It was quite a gathering. The cream of the free-lance crop, with only me to spoil the festivities . . . that is, if I could get in.

My eyes returned to the Countess, the undisputed belle of the ball. Her face was as unreadable as her Oriental counterpart. Whatever the physical pleasures of the previous day, my doubts about her were resurfacing.

She was now engaged in business, and where the Countess was concerned, that meant friends, lovers, even husbands, were pawns to be moved at will.

I had left her yesterday with some feeling of confidence. We had shared some sincerity, besides the lovemaking, during the afternoon. The new Countess was not the same viper the old one had been, and I felt I had reached her on some levels.

Once I had reported in, Hawk had helped to elevate those feelings. He was more convinced than ever that the bid was ours, and that the Countess could be trusted to honor her deal. Just to be sure, he said he would dispatch someone to watch her discreetly in the weeks after the auction. He again told me that I was to concentrate on Theo and leave the business end to him. I gave Hawk all the pertinent information on her hotel and room number, and trusted myself to the man's instincts.

That was, until this afternoon. I had joined the Countess at three o'clock, two hours before the appointed meet, to discuss the strategies that would gain me entry. For a lady as clever as she was, she had few suggestions.

We finally accepted the fact that she and I would have to bargain when the time came. Failing that, there was still the letter tucked in my pocket. My concern at the moment was that the letter was all the solution she really cared about. Once again, time would tell. I could only hope she would be persuasive.

Until then, there was only the tourists, and the wait. I checked my watch. It was 5:20, twenty minutes past zero hour. Theo was no doubt enjoying the anxiety he must have known he was generating. I sighed and turned back to the view. The time would pass soon enough.

It was a lapse of only minutes before the sound of footsteps roused the attention of all. I turned to see three men approaching, all dressed in suits, all with bulges beneath their coats where guns usually ride. Two of them stopped a short distance off, their hands hovering beneath their jackets, while the third stepped up to each of the candidates in turn.

His eyes drilled each member of the enclave until he was convinced of their identities. The last to be approached was the Countess.

I moved from the wall and drew up to them. I was ready to plead my case and test the Countess's commitment to our bargain.

I never got the chance.

The lady gestured in my direction and began to offer argument, but she was cut off as the man's booming voice addressed the assembly.

"You will all follow me, please. There will be a walk of some distance. To you, an inconvenience we regret. To us, an assurance that you have all lived up to your agreements."

I moved toward the man, clearing my throat as I prepared an argument of my own. But I, too, was cut off.

"Mr. Carter! You will, of course, join us?"

The shock of hearing my name, not to mention my inclusion in the soirée, was registered on the Countess's face as well as my own. I nodded numbly and followed, taking the Countess's arm as I passed. One by one the group filed in behind, with the two other gunsels pulling up the rear.

As we moved out of the courtyard, the Countess tossed me a whispered comment. "I thought you said you weren't invited!"

"I didn't think I was."

"Very odd, dear boy. I get the feeling your presence was very much anticipated."

"As I told you. The bid is ours. Just start counting your money, Countess. I'll handle the rest."

It wasn't my intention to be curt, but I wanted time
and silence to think. The Countess obliged. We stepped
out of the grounds and began moving down the hillside.
Almost immediately we turned down a cobbled street
and entered a section of the city known as the Alfama.

Theo could not have set it up any better.

The Alfama stretched out from beneath the castle,
the oldest quarter of the city. It is a veritable labyrinth
of narrow, twisting alleyways; a confusion of ancient
stone and stucco dwellings that seem to have situated
themselves like tumbling boulders from above.

We moved like rats in a maze, twisting and turning
through a route that would make pursuit easily detecta-
ble and memorization impossible.

At one moment we might walk a street alive with
activity—cages of canaries hung on exterior walls, wom-
en strolling by bent from the jugs of water perched atop
their heads—and then we would turn, descending the
hill on stairs so narrow the Countess would have to walk
in front of me.

Wherever we were being led, there would be only one
way back, and that was with guidance. The losers would
be led one way, the winner another. The twain would
never meet. Theo's game had all the earmarks of a fail-
safe show.

But attempting to memorize routes was the furthest
thing from my mind. What plagued me now was the
hard reality of the Countess's observation. My presence
seemed very much anticipated, and the knowledge of
that was chilling. Even with the realization that I was being led—run by the master himself—the whole thing
was still confusing.

How does a man put an assassin on your tail and then
expect you to show up at the ball? If he knew the attempts had all failed, he might expect me to try for the
auction, but why do you do your damnedest to stop

someone from showing—and then throw out the red carpet?

The questions rattled in my brain, but I knew I would soon have the answers. Our little parade came to an abrupt halt.

We stood before a cracked and scarred home, a stone crest above its opening a weathered tribute to some ancient aristocrat. The leader pushed open the door and mutely gestured us in.

We entered what was once the main room of the dwelling. It was musty and dark, lit only by the light of the front door and an open archway at the back. In the recesses of the room were three more men. None of the three wore suits, and all held machine pistols in full view.

Lining each side of the room were two wooden benches. As we entered, we were directed to sit. The Countess, Kiang, and I were placed on the right, the others across from us. Once we had settled, the rear guard entered, shutting the door behind them.

The leader broke the silence. "If any of you has brought weapons, you will please place them on the floor now."

He paused, but no one responded. With rapid-fire Portuguese, he directed two of the guards to conduct a search. As the men complied, he spoke again. "You are all here on a matter of business. The *senhor* upstairs wishes this business to be conducted in an atmosphere of honor. If any of you is found to have lied about weapons, you will be promptly returned to your vehicles."

Fortunately for all, the search proved fruitless. The man accepted the judgment of his cronies and continued. "I will now ask that each of you disrobe."

There was a flare of protest from the participants, but the man was adamant. "You will remove your clothes, or you will depart. The choice is yours."

When no one else spoke, I cleared my throat loudly

and offered my own opinion. "I thought the question here was honor. It seems we've established ours."

The man whirled in my direction and glared. "The question here is also safety. I am told that you yourself, Mr. Carter, are capable of fashioning weapons from the simplest of devices. Nudity provides a certain security, don't you agree?"

I did not. But I saw no reason in arguing the point. Whatever doubts still lingered in the room were quickly dispelled by the Countess. With a loud, booming, "Shall we get on with it!" she began peeling herself out of her clothes, the others hesitating only long enough to enjoy some of the sight before complying themselves.

When we were all bare-assed naked, the leader stepped back through the open archway, into what once had apparently been the cooking area. He called us through, one at a time, and diverted us to a stairway at the right. We each obliged, moving up the narrow risers to the second floor of the dwelling.

The upstairs room was far brighter, being lit by twin windows at both the back and front. The center was occupied by a huge table with seating for eight. In front of each of five of the chairs was placed a small envelope and pencil. A sixth chair remained with nothing on the table before it.

It was chairs six, seven, and eight that captured my attention. Five chairs, five envelopes, five bidders. The sixth chair had to be mine, the all-too-anticipated unexpected guest.

How could Theo have known?

Chairs seven and eight were occupied by the sources of my concern. They were the chairs of command, ruling from the head of the table.

In one sat Theo, his dark hair curled and shining, his face tanned and confident.

To his left sat the girl from Military Intelligence,

Leslie Solari. Both were clothed, both were fully in control of the situation.

As we entered, one by one, Theo pointed us to our seats. I was gestured to Leslie Solari's left, the Countess and the black man following. Down the opposite side came Alibaz to Theo's right, then Kiang, then Egerklein.

I used the time it took for all to sit to study the lady that Theo had so effectively subverted. Leslie Solari was not unattractive. She was severe, with an angular boniness that gave her an awkward thrust. Everything about her—face, shoulders, hips—all seemed to jut out at you but not without dignity. There was an aura of aristocracy to her.

The only part of her that seemed fluid was her eyes, especially as she watched Theo. I'm not a total authority on heavy relationships when it gets beyond a one-night stand. I don't have time, and involvement doesn't come with the territory. But my intuition told me that the girl was very much in love.

The room settled quickly, and all eyes riveted to the head of the table, a dramatic silence permeating the air. It was Theo's show and everyone knew it. And N1 was taking his time. Beginning at his right, his eyes circled the table, taking each person in turn.

Mine was the last face he settled on. His eyes dug into me, peeling back the layers of prepared indifference to try to fathom what lay beneath. I held the gaze, trying to uncover the enigma that was Theo.

Earlier I had hoped to get a reaction from the man. I had hoped that by surprising him, I could get a measure of his feelings about me. But that was impossible now. One could not make an impact when one was expected.

Theo terminated the contest with the faintest hint of a smile and the barest nod of his head. He then broke to address the room.

"Gentlemen," he announced, his deep voice modulated and full of civility, "and dear Countess. Welcome. My apologies for any inconvenience or embarrassment you have suffered at my hands. We have an unusual situation here, and I'm afraid it calls for rather unorthodox methods. As you well know, in our business information is usually gained in bits and pieces from a variety of sources and for a variety of motives. But it is usually done under fairly standard procedures."

The individuals around the table, wearing nothing but a blush, obviously held a quiet yearning for the familiarity of those methods. Theo noted it with a slight smile and moved on, gesturing to his lady as he did.

"What we represent is a defection and the subsequent theft of sensitive material on a scale as yet unprecedented in the annals of espionage. Our motives are strictly monetary, free of any allegiance to political philosophies. You are not strangers to each other. One look around the table will quickly confirm that each of you was invited for your own affinities. It was our intention that each of the world's major power blocs be represented."

Egerklein's hand lifted from the far end of the table. Theo acknowledged him with a nod. "Are we to assume then, that we are committed to the various blocs with which we are aligned?"

"Not at all, Herr Egerklein," Theo replied. "The mix present in this room merely represents the apolitical nature of our intent. It is also a kind of first guarantee that you are not being fed misinformation. There are no targeted recipients. The highest bidder will claim the prize."

Theo quickly motioned toward the Countess and myself as he talked on. "Even the Western interests, from whom the material was stolen, are represented. Money, and money alone, will determine the outcome. Beyond the events in this room, the fate of the material is a matter of complete indifference to me. You are all free to broker the information entirely as you see fit."

A faint but greedy grin lit the corners of the German's mouth. Visions of wealth were dancing behind his eyes, visions cut short by the halting, bass voice of the black across from him.

"You are certain the material is complete? We are not purchasing fragmented information?"

It was Leslie Solari who chose to answer. Her voice was official and firm, every inch the executive secretary she had been. But at the same time it was tempered with a surprising gentleness.

"You have all been given copies of my credentials at Military Intelligence. I am certain you have had the facts confirmed. You may rest assured that the material is quite comprehensive. There are no gaps."

The black gave a stiff nod of acceptance, while Alibaz jumped in with typical abrasiveness. "I accept the completeness of your material and the apolitical nature of your motives. But what guarantees do you offer as to authenticity? How do we know we are not buying a fiction?"

In spite of the man's tone, Theo greeted his comment with a smile. He turned to Leslie and gave her a brief nod. She reached down and lifted a small pile of manila folders onto the table.

From my vantage point, I could see that each folder had a name typed neatly across its face. Leslie rose and distributed them, making her way around the table in perfect succession.

For a brief few seconds I watched her, a chilling balloon of fear expanding in my guts with each step closer to me. As fear grew, doubt receded. There was no longer any question that I had been manipulated by the best, maneuvered into the chair I now occupied.

But I suddenly knew my purpose in being there.

Oh, there were still nagging questions . . . tiny ones
. . . like mosquitoes pecking at my flesh. Why the attempts on my life? Why lure me? Why not just invite me
like the others? But there was no longer doubt itself.

Only the pervading sense of defeat.

I looked over to where Theo sat. His eyes were riveted on me, delving, boring into me with incredible in-
tensity. He could sense the defeat, smell it, savor it.
There, spread across his face, was a knowing, sadistic
smile of victory.

The final folder was slapped down before me. My
eyes dropped down to scan the cover, and my worst,
most demoralizing fears were realized.

Across the face of the folder was written the name,
*Father O'Hanlon*. Below that, a personal, handwritten
message. *Thanks, Nick. I couldn't have sold them without you!*

# NINE

There was horror at the sight of those words. Like any of life's pursuits, espionage has its technical side. You train the body, you train the mind. You arm yourself with methods and weapons and all the assistance technology can offer, and dive out into the field. But none of these are any guarantee of success.

The edge, the *real* assets that separate the good from the brilliant agents, are purely psychological. In the long run, it's your ability to outthink, outpsych, and outmaneuver the enemy that keeps you from pushing up flowers in some potter's field.

A long-ago quote suddenly trickled its way into my numbed consciousness. *"It's a chess game, Nick. What you want to do is sit there with a pile of envelopes on your right hand, and every time the other guy makes his move, you want to be able to crack open the top envelope, and show him what he just did."*

The quote was Theo's. The folder I now stared at was grim confirmation that nothing I had done since day one had been anything but anticipated. I was merely a student, buried in the shadow of my teacher, listening as his words echoed through the room.

"Gentlemen," he said, "what you now have before you are samples. A minute but representative example of the quality of the goods you will receive. You should note that much of what has been stolen is quite technical. There are numerous graphs, charts, mappings—the kind of material that would take years to falsify. It is our intent to leave this room impossibly wealthy. I see no reason to sully that intent by earning it through labor, false or not. There will be no fictions."

Each of the table's occupants opened his brief and read in rapt excitement. The four or five pages each held before him was a small gold mine in its own right. That those papers represented only a fraction of the total set each mind to calculating in numbers that numbed the senses.

There was no need to open my own. I needed no guarantee as to the authenticity of the contents. It was their return that concerned me most. I shoved the folder aside and lifted my gaze to the man who held the outcome in such full control.

Theo was staring at me, a gloating smile creasing his face. It held until the rustle of papers being returned to their folders filled the room.

By the time Leslie had collected them and returned to her chair, Theo's attention had shifted from me back to his customers.

"As you can see, the material is quite genuine." He smiled. "If there are any lingering doubts, I will give you over to the ultimate authority. To my left is one of America's top agents. Although many of you may not know his face, I'm sure that all of you have heard the name at one time or another: Nick Carter."

The announcement brought a small murmur from the group. I glared at the audacity of the man.

"Forgive the reticence," he continued, with a nod in

my direction. "Mr. Carter is understandably silent because he is on a very delicate assignment. He has been given the unenviable task of retrieving his government's property. In that, he will take his chances with the rest of you. Beyond that, it is also his duty to punish me for my transgressions. It is for that reason I have been forced to subject you to certain precautions." Then he turned to me. "Have I misrepresented anything, Nick?"

"No," I hissed coldly. "I think that about covers it."

With a light laugh, Theo turned back to the others. "So you see, my friends, you may rest assured the material is pure gold. Shall we move on with it then? Before Mr. Carter terminates your source?"

There was a general round of assent from the table, interrupted by the gentle voice of Kiang. "Forgive my impertinence, but should Mr. Carter prove successful in the second phase of his mission, how will this affect the outcome of the bidding?"

Theo acknowledged the question with a polite bow of his head. "An intelligent point, Kiang. To answer you, not at all. Even should Mr. Carter be successful in his mission, which he won't be, a system of exchange for the material has been engineered in such a way that the buyer will have total protection. Protection from the offended government, from reprisals, and even—not to be rude—from any misguided zeal from the others in this room."

He stood and began pacing behind his chair. "I will share the outlines of this system with you all. I hope by doing so to discourage any of you from attempting any foolish enterprises. I consider this entire affair to be the highlight of my career, and I don't want that triumph marred by needless intrigue or bloodshed. The amount of material, as you can imagine, is vast. Out of necessity we were required to photorecord the information onto

computer discs, some three hundred in all. The material
you were given to examine were random photo repro-
ductions of the original material, so I can assure you the
quality will be indecipherable from the original." He
paused, his eyes flickering around the table. "Any questions to this point?"

There were none.

"Good, in that case let me continue. The discs were
then divided, again at random, into fifteen different
packages and placed in trust at fifteen different banking
institutions. The names and locations of those institutions will be made available solely to the winner of the
bidding. In turn, I will announce to each bank the identity of the top bidder, and he or she will be named as
beneficiary to the trust upon receipt of a sum equal to
one-fifteenth of the accepted bid.

"Within an hour of the completion of today's business, the given banks will have the data necessary to ex-
pedite transfer of the information in any manner you
may see fit. So, I assure you, any fate that may befall me
will in no way affect the outcome of the bidding."

There was a satisfied buzz around the table, and
Egerklein again cut nervously into the hum. "Will we be
able to examine the material before handing over the
money?"

For the first time, a note of irritation entered Theo's
voice. "*Naturlich, mein Herr!* But you would be a fool to
do so. If my sincerity has not yet been established to
you, then feel free to check at will. But I will say, for the
last time, the information is there, and it is genuine."

Egerklein did not fail to catch the tone. "Forgive me,
my friend. I did not mean to imply . . ."

But Theo was in no mood for fawning apologies. "Although the brilliance of what I am offering has no doubt
already occurred to most at this table, allow me to make

it clear for your benefit. What I have created for you, Herr Egerklein, is a safe repository for the information. If you so choose, you never even have to touch it. You have only to approach the government or governments of your choosing, sell the information piecemeal or intact, and have the trust transferred to their representatives upon receipt of any payment you have negotiated. It is *they* who then assume responsibility for the actual payment of money and the transfer of the discs." His stare was icy cold as he leveled it on the German. "Could anything be simpler, or safer, *mein Herr?*"

Egerklein's face flushed red. "*Nein, mein Herr.* My compliments on your thoroughness."

"I have a question of sorts, sir." It was Kiang.

"Yes?" Theo said, turning his attention to the Chinese.

"It is a system both elegant and simple. So elegant, in fact, that one wonders why you do not avail yourself of it personally."

Theo nodded and cast a quick glance in my direction. "You are quite correct, Kiang. My reasons for involving any of you are twofold. On the one hand, there is the apolitical facet of my intent. America deserves the right to regain its losses. Because of my defection, and the theft it entailed, I could not offer them that privilege without putting myself in jeopardy. Although one of you will end up possessing the material, you did not steal it, so you do not run the same risks. You are all internationals, safe from the jurisdiction of United States law."

"And the other factor?" Kiang prodded.

Theo paused a long moment before answering, then sighed. "There will be certain . . . stipulations . . . attached to the trust. Mr. Carter is living proof of the extent to which my government will go in reprisal. I will need time . . . time to vanish. I can ill-afford the kind of visibility any negotiations would entail."

Alibaz leaned forward intently. "You mean we will be forced to wait before we can negotiate?"

"No," Theo answered, shaking his head. "You are free to negotiate immediately. That in itself will occupy some time. It is the transfer process that I must force you to extend. In all, I am speaking only of a few months, enough time for me to relocate myself and take any necessary steps to secure my future. Are there any pressing timetables in this room that three months would cripple?"

All heads wagged in the negative.

"Thank you. If there are no more questions, I suggest we get on with the bidding."

There was a rustle of excitement as Theo moved back to the head of the table and sat down.

"The bidding will be handled thusly. Before each of you is an envelope and pencil. Inside the envelope is a printed card with your name on it. Below your name is a space upon which you will enter your bids. You will now take your envelopes and go downstairs. Each of you has been assigned one guard. You will be allowed to dress, and then you will be escorted to isolated quarters nearby. You may take as much time as you wish to consider your bid, but you will write one amount, and one figure only. The starting figure is two hundred and fifty million dollars, and the highest figure above that will win the bid. Have I made myself clear?"

Egerklein leaped in. "Are we to return here after the bidding?"

"Indeed not, my friend," Theo replied. "Only the winner will be summoned to return. The rest of you will be informed of your bad fortune and escorted by my men back to your respective hotels. I feel it is in the best interests of all concerned that the winning bidder be given as much security as possible."

"Why our hotels?" chimed Alibaz. "Our drivers are back at the castle."

"So they are. However, I'm sure you can see how easily one might wait and count the returning faces. One has only to count to four, and the identity of the winner would be instantly known. And there is always the possibility that your drivers are more than they seem. No, I want no surprises. The only fate that concerns you from this point on is your own."

There was a general air of discomfort around the table. One that was quickly dispelled by the Countess. "An admirable arrangement," she said, rising in her place. "You are to be commended." There was a reluctant but unanimous echo of her sentiments as all rose to go.

"And what about me?" I asked.

Theo turned to me, that emotionless smile still glued to his face. "You will go downstairs and dress. You may . . . confer with your associate if you so choose. You will then come back here to await the results. Paulo will escort you personally."

The man who had led the parade from the castle had silently appeared at the head of the stairs. With a nod to Theo I rose to join the departing guests.

Back downstairs, everyone dressed quickly. I took the opportunity to pull the Countess aside.

"Bid the minimum and not one penny more," I growled.

"Don't be a fool, Nicholas!" she flared. "Are you that anxious to gamble your country's fate on the supposed sentiments of a defector?"

"Defector, yes. But not a traitor. It's a closed ballot. No one will ever know the real figures. It's ours, Countess, I promise you!"

A low chuckle erupted from her throat. "Theo is no saint. He's a businessman, dear boy. All he cares about is money, as much of it as he can get!"

I grabbed her. "You're right, but he also wants to live to spend it. If that material finds its way in any direction but home, he'll have every agency of the U.S. government after his ass. He'll live what time he has left staring over his shoulder in fear. He knows there's no percentage in that. At least if the goods are returned home, there'll only be me to deal with. Trust me, Countess. The minimum—and nothing more! Am I clear?"

She studied me uncertainly. "You're convincing. But the question we must all concern ourselves with is, are you *right?*"

I released my hold on her. "I'm right, Countess. Believe it with all your heart."

She studied me a moment longer, then moved off to claim her escort. No sooner had she gone then Paulo tapped my arm and gestured me to return upstairs. I preceded him up the narrow stairway, a hundred questions forming themselves in my mind as I entered the room once more.

Paulo stationed himself at the stairs to my left, and to my right, Leslie Solari stared idly out the window. Theo sat in his chair at the end of the table, his expression arrogant, his voice deceptively gentle as our eyes locked on each other.

"Hello, Nick. Have you missed me?"

"Yeah, but only because I haven't gotten a clean shot at you," I retorted.

His responding laugh was only more of an irritant. "Bitter, are we? Dear me, I've sinned against the fold."

As I watched the man, the hundreds of questions that had haunted me suddenly paled. Only one remained.

"Why, Theo? *Why?*"

His eyes dropped to the table, and his hands came together in front of him. Several seconds passed before he answered.

"What can I say, Nick? You want simple answers. There are none."

"You must have had some reason."

"One reason? Why not ten . . . or a hundred? Maybe it's change of life. Maybe it's vanity. Perhaps boredom." He turned slightly in his chair and looked to where Leslie Solari stood at the window. "Love, perhaps." Then he turned back to me. "Or frustration, or challenge, or fear, or glory. Why pull it apart, Nick? Why not just call it money and leave it at that?"

"No," I countered. "Not money, Theo. Money's too easy. AXE has too many accounts stashed in too many places for that. You could have easily emptied them all and faded into oblivion. But you didn't. Instead you walked out with a truckload of sensitive files and left an organization full of dead bodies in your wake. It deserves an answer."

He nodded cautiously. "I suppose it does." Then abruptly he turned to Paulo. "Start your rounds. It is time we see how the bidders are doing." The man at the stairs gave me a nervous glance and shuffled his feet uncertainly. "Go, Paulo. I am in no danger," Theo said. "This man wants answers, not violence. Make your rounds."

Reluctantly, Paulo nodded and started down the stairs. When he was gone, Theo turned to me and smiled.

"The violence comes later, right, Nick?" He chuckled mirthlessly.

I ignored him and pressed for an answer to the all-important question. "*Why,* Theo?"

His hands gestured in resignation. "Where do I start? How about insanity? A world gone mad, Nick. And within that world, we—you and I—typify a profession even more insane yet. Hyperinsanity, if you will. Sooner or later, it has to take its toll."

"In what way?"

Theo lurched forward in his chair, his hands rapping onto the table. "Let's try futility for starters. We spend years plying our trade, and for what? We topple one South American dictator so another can rise to screw us. We raise up our own Mid-East potentate so some idiot fanatic can tear him down. We pour arms into NATO, and they elect Socialist governments. It goes on and on, Nick, and where's the sense? Where's the reason!"

"You know your questions have no answers, Theo," I growled. "But when has it ever been different?"

"Once!" came the reply. "There was another time, Nick. During the war . . . the OSS . . . when this whole goddamn sideshow began, there was a purpose, a meaning. Then it was Fascism. Even during the early days of the CIA there was an enemy you could understand. Communism hung out there like a shroud. Even later, when issues began to blur, there was still AXE. While the CIA was being castrated by the Freedom of Information Act that gave every jackass the right to poke around, AXE remained silent and buried. We made definitive decisions and had the balls to act on them. There was still a purpose, Nick."

"And you don't think there is now?"

The eyes grew sad. "No. Not anymore. There are no more enemies, no more clear-cut policies. Just unrelated incidents, single acts that serve only to convince ourselves that we exist. The greatest nation on earth, my friend, and we can't get fifty people out of one embassy, or one general out of terrorist hands."

The air around him crackled with bitterness. Although I couldn't entirely dispute his reasoning, I could still not accept it as a motive worthy of the crime.

"Bullshit, Theo," I growled, leaning forward until we were nearly eyeball to eyeball. "Of course the world's insane. It always has been. Ever since the first monkey propped himself up on his hind legs, picked up the nearest bone, and took a swing at his neighbor . . . just because he *could*. To you Hitler was a fiend; to millions of Germans he was a savior. The issues have never been anything but muddy, the causes self-serving. Maybe you're just getting too old to handle them."

There was a momentary jerk of his shoulders, then a jarring laugh as he settled back in his chair. "Old, is it? Well, maybe you're right, my boy. Maybe, indeed. But that only raises another possibility, doesn't it?"

"How so?" I asked, trying to follow his change of attitude.

"Vanity, Nick! Surely in all the years we've known each other, you've come to know that about me. Maybe in all those years there never really were any causes, just victories—carving my name into the espionage hall of fame, heh?"

"You were good, Theo. The best."

He shrugged. "But who'll know it? Ours is a secret world, you and I existing only in shadows. Maybe, with this little deal, I wanted to make one statement of my *own*. One gesture that did not include the good of country and organization. At least make a name among the small coterie who people our profession."

I shook my head in disbelief. "Vanity, Theo? A graveyard full of AXE agents, men you trained, and all for *vanity*?"

"Why not? Vanity . . . and boredom. I was withering behind a desk, training and sending out others for missions I was far more qualified to do. I need challenge, Nick, not mental exercise. I've lived with survival too long to give it up. Without the struggle, I was dead."

"Why didn't you just request active duty?"

"I said challenge," he barked, his eyes beginning to glow. "Real enemies, Nick. Not the rats that peck and burrow their way through the woodwork. They may be irritating, even difficult, but they are not a challenge!"

The meaning behind his words hit me with frightening clarity. "But AXE is? Is that it, Theo?"

He grinned. "Yes, my friend. AXE is the best. I should know; I built it. There lies the ultimate test."

I felt sick to my stomach. "And what challenge is there in taking on someone you've murdered first?"

"Not murdered," he said, his head shaking vehemently. "Hindered maybe, but not murdered! Hawk will rebuild, just as he did before. It would be stretching vanity into idiocy to think I could handle you all. But I did leave him one, didn't I? I left him you, Nick, because you are the best. There's my challenge, my bright little pupil. I have made my statement, thrown down my glove. And someday—not today but someday—you will come to call on that debt. Then we will see. I will either be free . . . or dead." He smiled dryly, his eyes boring into mine. "Which do you think, Nick? Which way will it go?"

A slow smile curved my own lips as I returned his gaze. "I have been an apt pupil, Theo," I replied. "And I intend to collect all my debts."

He opened his mouth as if to speak again, but from the head of the stairs came the cautious clearing of Paulo's throat.

"*Senhor* . . ."

"What is it, Paulo?" Theo asked.

"The bids, *senhor*." He extended a hand in Theo's direction. In it he held five envelopes.

The bidders had made their decisions.

"Excellent," Theo rasped. He jumped from his chair and grabbed the envelopes from Paulo, then moved to the base of the table, tearing at the first one.

Leslie moved over to join him as, one by one, the envelopes were read. My position at the table made it impossible for me to determine which was whose.

In the end, one card remained in his hand. He showed it to Leslie, who eyed it, studied him uncertainly, and finally nodded her assent. Without a word being spoken, the name was shown to Paulo, and then the remainder of the bids were swept up and given over to the messenger. He was sent off with a terse order from Theo.

"Burn the bids, and inform the winner."

Paulo trotted off dutifully while Theo patted his sides in satisfaction. Leslie moved over to her chair and sat. Theo remained in place, his eyes beaming at me.

"So, my friend, enough of the past. Enough of motives, and theories. What of the future, eh?"

"My future, at the moment, appears to be in your hands, Theo," I said dryly.

Theo shook his head chidingly. "As a member of this auction, you will be given the same considerations as the others. I run an honorable show, Nick. You surely know that."

"Then you'll have your challenge. I promise you. And you can do me the favor of passing that on to your assassin. Tell him for me that he's a dead man."

Theo smiled at the comment, bowed his head, and began strolling around the table toward me. "Any ideas yet as to who he is?"

"Not by name. But that's only a matter of time. That little setup you arranged Friday is pretty solid proof that we both know what can be expected out of him. Drop him, Theo. He's too careless to provide you any protection. Keep him around, and he'll only blow you wide open."

Theo sat down on the table to my left, his arms folded across his chest. "Perhaps you're right, Nick. Takes some of the sport out of it, doesn't it. Would it help you at all if I gave you his name?"

My brows furrowed in confusion at this new wrinkle. Theo was obviously throwing away the rule book when it came to this encounter. "But why. . . ?"

He threw back his head and roared. "Bravado, Nick. Nothing but bravado! The name will be useless to you. You'll never get him, my friend, because he never was. I'm a selfish man. I didn't want to share you with anyone. It's me, Nick! It's always been me, from the moment the whole affair began!"

The words pounded into my gut like a fist. "But you sold out the others! And the bomb, the bomb in my apartment . . ."

"I had to sell out the others. I needed some room to operate, and I needed money to do it. But not you, Nick. You're mine. I planned out the bombing, and the incident at the airport, and the setup in the bar the other night. Then I hired independents to carry them out."

Again there was the one all-pervading question. "Why? You obviously wanted me here at the auction. Why the roadblocks to get here?"

"It's been a long time since we've worked together, Nick. I knew how good you were, but I had to see how good you've become. Besides, one gets a little rusty after years behind a desk. I needed to work my way back into the game."

"And what if one of the independents had succeeded?"

Theo shrugged. "Then you wouldn't have been that good, would you? Where would my challenge have been then?"

It all appeared sickeningly clear. So far the game was

all Theo's. All my planning, all my thinking, every move, had all been grist for Theo's mill. So far my presence had proven to be little more than a refresher course for the man I was forced to hunt down.

I was eating crow and choking on it.

But I was doing something else, too. I was committing. I was taking any doubts that had been hampering me and burying them forever. There would be no more battles with the past, no more agonies over the man I had known. He was letting me walk out of the auction and inviting me into the arena. It would be a whole new ball game.

Just him and me.

And I would take him.

I looked up to find him staring at me, his eyes gentle, almost compassionate, as though he had been able to read the battle that had just waged inside me.

"How do you feel?" he asked.

The answer came of its own accord. "Ready. How about you?"

The smile returned to his face. "Like I've just been reborn. The best of luck, Nick. The best of luck!"

Behind him came the sound of footsteps. The auction's winner had arrived. With a final wink of his eye, Theo stood to greet the victor. As he rose, my view opened to the head of the stairs. Whatever feelings of elation Theo's challenge had generated were just as quickly smashed as I gazed at the room's newcomer.

There, smiling beneficently around the room, stood the squat figure of Kiang.

# TEN

There are limits to the amount of manipulation the human psyche can tolerate. I had swallowed all the humility I could stomach. That Theo had controlled the battle so far was enough to handle. That my own instincts had betrayed me was more than I could endure.

It was just not possible that Theo would let that material get into enemy hands! It was insanity to its most ludicrous extreme. I shot a glance toward the defector, feeling capable at that moment of tearing him to pieces.

But the look on Theo's face brought me up short. He was obviously no more comfortable with what he was seeing than I was. For the first time, there was a visible crack in his omnipotent shell. Another quick look, this time to Leslie, confirmed the suspicion.

Kiang was there without invitation.

"What the hell are you . . . ?" Theo began, and then his face turned chalk white.

I whirled in the Oriental's direction, and my guts did a half-gainer.

We were all staring up the perforated barrel of a Czech ZK-466 machine gun.

"My apologies for this unexpected intrusion." He smiled with a slight bow.

"Don't be a fool, Kiang," Theo hissed.

The benign grin crumbled from the Oriental's face. "It is you, I'm afraid, who have been foolish. You mock us with your talk of honor—and then deal with the dog who comes to kill you! The dog and his bitch!"

The gun swiveled uncomfortably in my direction.

"Hold it, Kiang," I growled. "I'm a prisoner here. There are no deals. The bids are in, and I'm as ignorant as you of the outcome."

There was a tightening of his grip around the gun. "You lie!"

I looked quickly to Theo. "What the hell's going on?"

His only response was to lift his hand to silence me. The Oriental appeared to glean some kind of understanding in the gesture, because his tenseness seemed to drain. The barrel drooped only a few inches, but it was enough to give me a sense of reprieve.

"Perhaps you speak the truth," he said uncertainly. "But this is still a room of lies."

Through it all, Theo remained silent. In response, I asked the obvious question. "In what way, Kiang?"

When it came, his answer was directed at Theo, not me. "There is an odor to deceit. Very subtle, like the scent of the carnivorous Westerner. This room stinks of it. But there is subtlety also in the mind of the Easterner . . . like a many-faceted ruby!"

"Where is Ziad?" Leslie interjected.

"He sleeps," came the answer. "You have only your treachery to thank for that. I was content to honor your wishes, but I cannot honor your infidelity!"

"Why are you so certain you've been deceived?" I hissed, feeling the anger rising inside me.

Again it was Theo to whom the answer was directed. "It is beyond the power of the Occidental to ever fathom the Oriental mind. Your guard could lead me through a hundred mazes, and I would still clear my mind and remember. So I followed him, speaking with my mouth but learning with my senses. And when your man came to claim my bid, I let him go. But I silenced the guard, took his weapon, and returned to watch . . . to test the sincerity of your so-called honor." And then a laugh filled with contempt burst from him. "Honor! The bids flew home, like five tiny sparrows, but when your man again went out, it was not to me. You have left me with no choice. What you will not give me in honor, I will take with force!"

Theo finally broke his silence. "You speak like a philosopher, Kiang. You talk of honor and fidelity as though they were part of your daily trade. You're a spy, my friend, and an amateur at that. And though your mind may be a many-faceted jewel, it is one I find all too conveniently polished. There's more than one back out there that has tasted the sting of your honor!"

Kiang's hands again tensed around the gun, and his voice was low and guttural when he spoke. "Enough of words. I will have what is mine. You will hand to me the information I require, and you will notify those you must that I am the beneficiary of your trust."

"And if I refuse?" Theo said calmly.

Kiang had had his fill of words. The gun swiveled with sudden vehemence, and his finger gave a quick squeeze to the trigger. The chair to Leslie Solari's right burst into fragments. She screamed and threw herself to the left as Theo's voice burst through the gunfire like a cannon.

"Enough! We shall do as you ask!" he barked.

From his coat pocket he produced an envelope and slid it across the tabletop. Kiang watched it hungrily as it slid to a halt before him. He moved forward and grabbed it, his fingers flickering almost lovingly over its surface.

"You are wise," he smiled. "You have redeemed yourself." And then his eyes fell on me. "Perhaps I can reward you for your cooperation. Perhaps I can rid you of the plague that follows you."

The gun turned in my direction and leveled itself at my chest. I don't really know what it was I expected out of that moment. Irony, I guess. Thoughts of Theo's precious challenge ending at the hands of another filled me with an inner angry frustration.

But what I got instead was Theo's firm and chilling voice, the same voice that had turned Julio Martinez's blood to ice, the voice that steals your will.

"If you are going to pull that trigger, now would be as good a time as any."

The room exploded with a single blast. For me time dropped to a crawl, a slow-motion hell. In spite of every instinct to the contrary, my eyes did not shut, my body did not retreat. Instead, I watched my expected death like a casual spectator. My eyes traced the bullet from the gun, watching it as it left the barrel and spiraled toward my chest. Such is the brief mirage of one's own demise.

That the bullet found its target was painfully evident in the bursting of the chest, the billowing ribbons of flesh and fabric that exploded like a final fanfare over the table. What gave me the greatest satisfaction was that the chest was Kiang's . . . not mine.

The man jerked, his eyes bulging in horror, death sending its final message to all of those finely honed senses. And then he toppled, pitching forward, his face slamming onto the table. The last to go were the knees, and as they bent to the final reality, the man slid slowly to the floor.

Behind him, her hair torn from its perch atop her

head, a tiny pistol smoking in her hand, stood the Countess.

"There's nothing more tedious than a poor loser," she said.

"And nothing more refreshing than a winner," Theo grinned.

The Countess gave a quick glance at Kiang's body. "Dear, dear Kiang. He did seem put out. What made him so certain he had won?"

"His bid," Theo answered. "One penny higher than the highest."

A faint slip of a smile cracked the Countess's lips. "Ah! The Oriental mind."

My eyes fell on the machine gun lying at the Oriental's feet. I drifted slowly toward it but came to a halt at the firm command of the Countess's voice.

"I'd rather you didn't, my dear sweet boy." I looked up to see the barrel of her gun aiming right between my eyes. "Nothing rash, remember?"

The Countess stepped up, claimed the gun, and slid it down the table's length to Theo. "Yours, I believe." She then lifted the envelope from where it had fallen on the table and, like the man before her, weighed it with her fingers. "Mine, I believe."

There was a smile in Theo's response. "An honor, Countess. Always an honor."

She tucked the envelope into her handbag and began moving the pistol up toward her hair. Her motion halted as Theo questioned her. "Your own design, I take it?"

"One of the fringe benefits of the arms trade," she said with a grin, obvious pride in the response. "You get to invent." She held the gun for all to see. "A simple two-shot derringer, modified to my specifications, of course. Small, light, easy to conceal, but it can knock the ass-end off an elephant at fifty yards."

With that, her hand continued, the weapon resting on her head, her hair lifting back up to conceal its presence.

"Don't be angry with me, Theo," she said as she worked. "In spite of all Kiang's philosophy, we're basically a grimy lot. One must always be prepared. Don't you agree?"

"What about Cleante?" Leslie asked.

"The guard?" she said, her hands giving a final pat to her coif. "A sweet boy. He was so enamored of my perfume, I gave him a special whiff from the bottle. He should awaken any minute now. Quite unharmed, I assure you."

"And Paulo?" added Theo.

"A less kind fate, I'm afraid. Mr. Kiang was quite merciless in his anger. I found the body on my trek back here."

Leslie's voice seemed slightly incredulous. "You anticipated trouble?"

The Countess smiled in my direction before answering. "Nicholas assured me the bid would be ours at the minimum figure. It was an assurance that gave me great doubt, but . . . in the end . . . I took him at his word." She then turned back to Theo. "But, while I may trust him, I wouldn't dream of extending that courtesy to the others. In business, my dear Theo, one always anticipates trouble. You would do well to heed that in the future."

Theo's laughter split the room. "I will, Countess, I assure you I will!"

"Good." She nodded a few times, then continued right on with the business she was so good at. "I have the lists. I assume there is also some sort of timetable I am to follow?"

"It's in the envelope," Theo replied as he rounded the table toward her. "I'll notify the banks today that you are assuming responsibility for the accounts. They will transfer the trust to you on the specified dates—or any time thereafter—and upon receipt of the agreed-on figures. Congratulations. You and your associate are free to go."

I stood up, ready to depart with the lady . . . but froze as her next words echoed through the room. "You did mean what you said earlier, didn't you? I *am* free to broker the material as I see fit?"

Even Theo was caught off guard. The smile faded from his face, and he glanced quickly over to me. The look he saw was one of total disbelief. The Countess too looked over, her answering comment of little relief. "Business, Nick. You understand?"

Theo remained silent, his mind apparently unsure of how to answer. That Hawk had been right about him was never more evident. He wanted the material to go home. That Hawk had misjudged the Countess was equally evident. She viewed the silence as her own personal consent.

"Very good," she trilled. "I do so adore doing business with honorable men. They're so easy to snow! Now, if one of you would be so kind as to point out my way home, I shall leave you to yourselves . . ."

At that moment she was interrupted by the sound of panicked feet leaping up the stairs. The Countess's guard, Cleante, his head still slightly fuzzy from her "perfume," stumbled into the room. He came to an abrupt halt, staring from one to the other of us as he tried to determine what the hell was going on.

"Ah! Cleante! Good to see you again!" the Countess chirped as she waltzed over and patted his cheek. Then she turned back to Theo. "Never mind. My guide has arrived." She linked her arm through Cleante's and beamed. "Shall we go?"

The dazed guard looked to Theo, awaiting his orders. All he got in response was a reluctant nod.

"Countess, don't do this!" I hissed. "We have a deal!"

Her head spun to where I stood, and her look was chilling. "Sue me," she said, her smile like ice. "But I really must thank you, dear boy. I couldn't have bid that low without you. Do delay him, won't you, Theo?"

With a wave of her hand, she led Cleante down the stairs and was gone.

I turned to Theo. He only shrugged. "Sorry, Nick. I can't control every turn of the cards. Leslie, why don't you take off and notify the banks. I'll wait until Cleante returns, and then I'll join you."

Leslie moved to where he stood and gently caressed his cheek. "All right, darling. And I'll start putting . . ."

But Theo cut her off. "You know what needs to be done, my love. I'll be there shortly."

She nodded and disappeared down the stairs.

Theo watched her depart, then he turned to me. The gun was slung casually from his arm, his distance from me obviously calculated to avoid temptation. "Nick, about the Countess . . ."

"I'll get her, Theo. Her and the goods."

There was a slight pause. "Of course. But I did want to warn you of . . ."

"Of what? . . . Treachery?" I growled. "No need, Theo. I've already seen the master at work."

He sighed heavily. "I can't deny you your hatred, Nick. But isn't it possible to be adversaries without being enemies? We have a lot of years between us."

"Ancient history, Theo. When you packed and ran, you left a lot of dead bodies behind you. And our friendship."

He shrugged and began breaking down the gun in his hand. He popped a fresh clip into the chamber, checked the trigger mechanism, then laid the reassembled weapon across his lap.

At that moment, Cleante returned. Theo spoke to him in hushed tones, then moved to the stairs. At the door he turned, facing me squarely, his voice low and intense.

"You don't want to hear it, Nick, but you're going to. Shut it out if you wish, but you must hear it! This is something I *had* to do. There was no luxury of choice. You can't have had the career I did and content yourself with cranking out little copies of yourself. It was like a living death . . . a slow and painful erosion of the soul. At least this way, death, if it should come, will be quick and, I hope, with dignity. I'm all there is facing you, Nick. There will be no assassins, no independents. Just me. I want to face you the same way. I don't want your friends from MI-6 involved."

At the mention of them, the hair on the back of my neck bristled as the horror of having exposed Jamie and Belinda washed through me once more. My eyes bored into Theo's, and he nodded.

"Just you and me, Nick. The *challenge!* Just the way it should be."

He inclined his head toward the guard, now sitting casually on the table's edge across from me. When he spoke again, it was in Greek. It was a language I understood, but Cleante, apparently, did not.

"I have ordered him to wait ten minutes before he kills you," Theo said matter-of-factly, and then he smiled. "I have no doubts that he will fail. Give me two minutes. Once you have freed yourself, get to a phone and warn your friends from MI-6. The hit has already been ordered. It's too late to reverse it now, but there's a chance you can reach them in time. Warn them and then send them home. You and me, Nick. Agreed?"

I took a deep breath, then nodded. "You've got your challenge, Theo."

Theo stared at me for one more brief moment, then turned on his heel and disappeared down the stairs.

I glared at the empty space where he had been, allowing the promise I had just made to brand its way into my brain.

The next thing I did was promptly break it.

No sooner had Theo reached the floor below then I moved. My head twisted toward the guard. He sat on the table's edge, one foot hitting the floor, the other propped up on the table. The gun rested loosely in his hands.

In one swift move I twisted my body, planted my feet and hands, and rose up with every ounce of body strength I could muster. My side of the table rose with me. The guard had only the time it took for realization to hit before his perch dropped out from beneath him.

To his credit, he did try. He threw his weight onto his right foot in an attempt to hurl himself away. But he wasn't in position. His heel slid across the floor, and he slammed down onto his back. Again he tried, doing his damnedest to swing the gun in my direction. But panic was now gripping him. His finger squeezed reflexively against the trigger, sending a shower of gunfire that tore holes in the ancient ceiling.

By the time the gun was anywhere near where it could have done me harm, I had already pressed my way forward, dropping the table over the top of him with a vengeful crash of wood. Still his finger demanded action, the bullets retracing their way across the ceiling and eating their way into the far wall.

I quickly lifted to my feet and kicked at the table's underside. I screamed, slamming my feet into the wood, supporting and encouraging the man's panic until the gunfire ceased, and the impotent click of the empty clip announced the end.

Just as quickly, I reached down and dragged the table aside. The guard tried to rise, but three quick blows to his throat put an end to his efforts. And his life.

I searched and found a spare clip in his rear pocket, my mind racing as I slammed the clip home. The stairway was too slow. Instead I slung the gun's strap over my head, raced to the window, hoisted myself through, and dropped to the cobblestones below. I hit the ground and crouched, my head dropping to let the gun slip off.

By the time I gripped it and rose up, I could see Theo running about thirty meters ahead. He was nearing one of the alleyways, his body angling for a right turn and safety.

I threw myself to the left, opening the angle of fire. Even as the first blasts of my attack sent stucco and stone chipping from the wall behind him, he did what only Theo would do.

He changed direction and dove through the opening to his left. I did my best to follow, but I had already committed. I let up on the trigger and bolted toward the alleyway. By the time I reached it and centered myself for another fusillade, he was nowhere to be seen.

I held both my position and my breath, listening for the faintest hint of a noise. Seconds ticked by before I was rewarded. There came a sudden screeching wail and a dart of movement. I fired.

I scrawny calico cat lifted from the impact of my rage and slammed down onto the street, a lifeless bag of fur, all nine lives torn from him in the blink of an eye.

I stared at the carcass and cursed under my breath as I considered my options. I could move into the alley, pursue the man I would kill with pleasure, but I might waste precious time. This was his setup, and he knew all the routes.

I could also make for the Countess. The material was, after all, the number one priority. But Hawk had promised watchdogs, and I would be wasting time to challenge that promise. That left my friends from MI-6.

There were no decisions. I couldn't let them suffer the consequences of my errors.

I let the gun slip from my hands and turned, breaking into a dead run as I moved down the hill, my eyes searching for a phone.

I had to reach them in time. I had to!

My eyes shot skyward and seized upon the nearest length of cable I could locate. It hung suspended above me, and I followed its course, my fists pounding at the door of the house it fed into.

A frightened, weathered face responded, and finally yielded to my staccato bursts of Portuguese.

I grabbed at the phone and quickly dialed the number, my heart sinking with each unanswered ring.

"Please! *Please!*" I demanded of the receiver. "Answer! Now! Now, dammit!"

But the ringing at the other end possessed its own destiny, and it tapped out its inevitable message with metered efficiency.

There was not going to be any answer.

# ELEVEN

It was nearly eight o'clock by the time I reached the Hotel Plaza, and I knew the news was grim from the first second I hit the lobby. The desk clerk and one of the hotel attendants were in heated debate over the relative worthlessness of one of their employees. It seems the man had proven himself to be derelict by deserting his job mid-shift.

I could have told them that the man was no doubt still on the premises, probably dead and populating some little-used closet or corner of the basement. But that was for them to discover. What the argument told me was that whoever he had been, he had possessed passkeys.

I moved casually through the lobby and over to the service stairs. Once through the door, I took the five flights to Jamie's room at a gallop. I hit the fifth floor and gave the hall a brief look.

It was empty.

I moved quickly to the door of 509, not at all surprised by the ring of keys that hung from its lock. I pushed open the door and stared in. The room was dark, lit only by the outside glow of the setting sun. My eyes adjusted and were suddenly drawn to two pairs of feet. One pair dangled down from atop the mattress, and one pair

137

jutted up from the floor on the other side of the bed.

Both were stiff and deadly white.

I walked slowly into the room, the man on the bed coming into fuller view. Jamie lay stretched out, his body naked, his back riddled with holes. There was no need to go any farther. Belinda would only look the same.

I slumped into a nearby chair and fought off the self-hatred that wanted to take me. It would have been too easy to blame myself. True, I had let Jamie expose himself, but he had allowed it to happen. We all knew Theo was good. In this business you take your shots, and sometimes the other side comes up the winner.

So far, Theo had come up with nothing but plusses.

But that was to be a thing of the past. I stared once more at Jamie's lifeless form.

"By God," I whispered, "you damn well deserved better. I can't give you that. But Theo deserves much worse, and that I can give you!"

I turned and stepped through the adjoining door to room 510. It too was dark, but there was enough light to see that the room had been searched. I started toward the wall switch, intent upon surveying the damage, when something caught me hard on the back of the head.

I dropped to the floor, my eyes spinning from the blow, my mind bent on staving off the unconsciousness that wanted so much to envelop me.

I rolled onto my back, my hands reaching out defensively, and through the hazy fog that swirled around my eyes, I found myself staring up into the bulbous end of a silenced pistol.

"The challenge, Theo! Where's the challenge?" I rasped, and awaited the end.

But the end did not come. There was only silence.

And then the pistol dropped from view and a face loomed out from the fog, its features clearing as it neared.

"Jesus!"

It was a female voice.

I stared, uncertain of whether or not I had already passed on. I hadn't heard the gun spit, nor had I felt the sting of its bullet. Yet I could not be alive and still see what I was seeing.

The face was Belinda's.

I let my body slump. There was no point in fighting. I was either dead and reunited, or alive and in safe hands. Either way I had to get the cobwebs cleared from my brain.

The apparition went, then returned. A cold compress settled over my brow, and a warm hand caressed my cheek.

It took a few seconds, but sanity quickly returned.

I threw off the compress and stared again. The face refused to change. It was indeed Belinda, quite alive and quite beautiful. There was only the faintest puffiness around her eyes to mar that beauty.

"You are the proverbial sight for sore eyes," I murmured. "I thought that was you in there. What happened?"

She gave a deep sigh before answering. "Can you make it to your room? There's liquor in there."

I nodded and let her help me up. The knees felt as solid as mashed potatoes, and my head still buzzed a tune that was decidedly off-key, but the thought of a stiff scotch perked me up considerably.

"You all right?" she asked. I grunted. "Good. You go in and fix us up. I need to snap on some lights."

I wobbled into my room, and by the time I had fixed two doubles, Belinda had joined me. She plopped down on the edge of my bed and accepted the drink. I could see that she'd been crying.

"Now, start filling in the gaps," I said, settling myself next to her.

She took a long pull of scotch, took a deep breath, then let it out slowly. "Jamie went down to the coffee shop this morning and managed to hit up on one of the hotel birds. Some English girl on holiday, I think. With you heading out for the auction, Jamie knew there would be some dead time, so he set up a little tête-à-tête. The girl was traveling with chums, so he invited her up . . . just a spot of in and out, he thought."

"And?"

"The bird arrived, and the two of them went at it. The surveillance system was on, of course, and I did get a chuckle or two watching for a bit, but that really isn't my style so I slipped off for a bit of food, and let them have their laughs."

I looked over at the tiny monitor that the two had rigged to watch their rooms. Each room had several cameras to cover them, each one controlled by the unit's channel dial. The set was tuned to Jamie's room, but mercifully it was focused on the hall and door . . . the passkey removed, the door now firmly shut.

"I took my time about it," Belinda continued, "and when I got back, I checked the progress of events, as it were. That's when I saw it. Camera two was on, just like I had left it, only there wasn't any more playing going on. Just them. Like you found 'em."

My hand came up to rub her neck. Her eyes were riveted to the floor. They were full of sadness, but there were no more tears.

"Did you go in?" I asked.

"Started to," she said. "I got as far as the adjoining door and just couldn't make the step. Instead, I came

back here, and just sat . . . staring at the screen. There's
something about that screen that just makes it all so
make-believe. Like someone will run in, yell 'Cut,' and
everyone will get up and wipe the fake blood off their
bodies.'' She heaved another deep sigh. "But no one
yelled anything. Then the entry light blinked, and I
switched over to the door camera. There were no lights
on, and all I saw was your silhouette. I'm sorry, Nick. I
thought maybe they were coming back for me."

I shook my head. "They won't come for you, Belinda.
They don't have to. They've already killed you."

Her forehead wrinkled in confusion.

"Theo sent them," I explained. "He wants to face me
alone . . . no help from the British. And as far as the
goons who did it are concerned, they achieved that. The
only one Theo ever saw was Jamie. Any girl in Jamie's
room would be assumed to be you."

"But why does he want you alone? He's got his
bloody assassin, doesn't he?"

I shook my head. "There never was one. It was Theo
all along. He was leading me, throwing a few darts in my
face to keep me busy, but just sort of sizing up the competition. Theo wants it man-to-man, and I'll promise
you what I just promised Jamie. He'll get it, and it'll be
the last thing he'll ever do."

She reached up and gently ran her fingertips across
my forehead. "You still don't look in such great shape,"
she murmured.

"My sweet," I said, taking her hand and kissing it
lightly, "your prescribed medicine has worked wonders
already. And we've got things to do. We need to catch
up with the Countess, and fast. She—"

"Nick! The telly!" Her voice was a hoarse whisper as
she jerked her hand away and pointed to the screen.

I looked over. The unit was blinking frantically, a

tiny bulb in its upper right that told us someone was trying to enter 510.

"I thought you said they wouldn't come for me!"

"They won't," I answered. "But I didn't say they wouldn't come for *me*."

I leaped for the unit, turning the dial and settling the image from the camera that covered the door. There was a two- or three-second delay, and the door creaked cautiously open. A man peered through, satisfied himself of the room's vacancy, and then slipped in, sealing the door quietly behind him. From an inside pocket in his coat he withdrew a revolver. From his side pocket, a silencer. He placed the two together and drifted into the room.

I barked a quick command to Belinda. "Get me my playmates."

She promptly fetched Wilhelmina and Hugo from the dresser drawer. I switched the dial again, changing the angle to cover him uprighting one of the chairs and setting it in a corner of the room.

As I watched, I strapped Hugo to my arm. Then I held out my palm. Wilhelmina came to rest in it, her silencer already in place.

"Good girl!" I whispered, my compliments meant for both the lady and the weapon.

In the meantime, the intruder had found his way back into the hall and had killed the room's lights.

"And that's all you're going to kill," I muttered as the screen went black. I turned to Belinda. "Douse the lights—it's time to go hunting."

I slid over to the adjoining door and grasped the handle. By now the sun had set, and Belinda threw the room into total darkness. I raised the knob and slid open the door that faced onto our side. I placed my ear to the other room's section and listened. There were padded footsteps, and then I heard the sound of squeaking leather. The man was set up in his chair. All he needed now was company.

Belinda dropped down next to me and whispered, "We should take him alive, Nick. He may know something."

I considered the wisdom of her comment but dismissed it. Theo had shown me his methods. He had hit me with bombings and assassinations and traps . . . and all had proven to be nothing more than fakes. He had hired his men and watched them die, all in the name of studying me—all for the purpose of guiding me.

Why should this man be any different?

Theo wanted his showdown, just the two of us. He had proven it by tipping me to the hit on Jamie and Belinda. "Too late to call the hit off," he had said.

Then it also held true that he was too late to call off the pigeon sitting in the other room. The man was meant to talk to me. Of that I was certain. He didn't know it. He didn't have to. His job was to fail. But somewhere—either on him or by the very choice of him—Theo had planted a message, a message that required no words to speak.

All very subtle, all designed for good old Nick to figure out on his own . . . as though it was *his* idea.

Ah, the devious mind of the spy!

I gripped Belinda gently by the shoulders. "Sorry, luv, but we have to waste this one, and I'll need your help." I whispered my commands, and she nodded.

She moved away and slipped quietly out the front door. A second or two passed until I heard her bang away at the entrance to the other room. Her voice, thick with the lilt of an accent, was audible even through the adjoining barrier.

"Hey, open up! I'll be damned if I'm going to be stood

up by the bloody likes o' you!" There was more banging, followed by another screech from Belinda. "Don't play out-to-lunch with me. I saw your bloody back go creepin' in the bloody door, you damn bloody slug! I'll give ya thirty seconds to open this door. If ya don't, then I'm goin' to the bleedin' management!"

She punched the threat with a slam of her foot against the door. And then came silence, a silence I hoped she was using to clear away. From inside the room, I could hear the uncomfortable nervousness of a man as he squirmed in his chair, uncertain of what to do.

"Ten seconds!" came the shrill cry.

There was more squirming, and then the man stood.

"Twenty . . . you bastard!"

He moved uncertainly but steadily toward the sounds that plagued him. By the time Belinda had screamed out her "Thirty!," he had drawn up next to the adjoining door.

I rammed my shoulder into it, sending it flying open and him flying against the bed.

The end came swiftly. I pumped three rapid slugs into his body, and all motion ceased. I then ran to the door, snapping on the room's lights as I went.

I hit the door three times in rapid succession with my gun butt. That was Belinda's cue to get back into 511.

"Aw, the hell with you!" she cried for the benefit of any who may have overheard.

I ran back to look over the body and begin my search, pausing only to shout my orders to Belinda when she appeared at the door between the two rooms.

"Call MI-6 and get a clean-up crew over here. We're going to have to check out, and we don't want any scandals left behind."

"Right!" she said, and disappeared.

I studied the man's face. No memories. No triggers.

He was a stranger. If Theo had a message, it was planted on him somewhere. I riffled through the man's clothing, digging through the pockets, my eyes intent on any object seemingly out of the ordinary.

I found it quickly, almost too quickly. In the right-hand pants pocket was a small medallion. I debated for a moment whether or not I might be outpsyching myself. It could very well be the man's own charm. But then I discounted that. If it were his, it would be on a chain and he would be wearing it.

It was the plant. I could just hear Theo, in low, conspiratorial tones, setting the sucker up.

"After you've killed him, place this over his head . . . or his eyes . . . or his mouth . . . any obvious place. It will be a warning to others!"

I studied the medallion more closely, trying to find the meaning Theo intended for me to see. It was gold, one side occupied by a stylized rooster in side view, the other side an oddly spired building, perhaps a silo or a shed of some sort.Neither image conjured any immediate response, so I tossed the amulet into my pocket and finished searching the dead man. There were no other clues to be found.

I returned to 511. Belinda was already tossing what few goods she needed into a small overnight bag. I ran around tossing in my own. There was no need to load ourselves down with luggage. The one bag would do for essentials; MI-6 would take care of the rest. We gave the room a quick check to be sure that all the vitals were taken care of.

By the time we were satisfied, there came a measured knock at the door. Belinda answered it and received the necessary answers. The MI-6 crew stepped into the room, and we grabbed our bag to step out. We were halted only by the concerned voice of the crew master.

"You want to leave a forwarding address?" he asked. "Home office may need to locate you."

Belinda looked to me for an answer, and I grinned.

"The Ritz! Where else?"

The man tossed us a disgusted sigh and waved us out. As we went, I could hear him share the comment with his cronies, then the resulting laughter. I shook my head. To them it was just a joke.

To me, it was a pressing reality.

# TWELVE

It was close to ten o'clock before we reached the Hotel Ritz. I had the cabdriver stop half a block away, and Belinda and I walked the remaining distance. No sooner had we reached the door than I froze in my tracks.

Inside the lobby, his squat frame plastered against the main desk, stood Gustav. Behind him were three bags. The Countess had apparently decided to check out. I gave the lobby a quick sweep, looking for signs of anyone who might be interested in the Prussian's activities.

If Hawk had his watchdogs in place, they were certainly not visible.

I turned quickly to Belinda. "See the guy at the counter . . . the short, pudgy one?"

She nodded.

"Get to him. I don't care how you do it, but don't let him out of here. Get him away from that desk and back up to the Countess's suite as fast as you can."

A coy smile curved her pretty lips. "No problem. I haven't met a man yet that I can't get into a hotel room."

"This one wears perfume."

Her smile didn't falter. "Then I'll invite him up to trade makeup tips."

I chuckled and gave her arm a squeeze. "Now get in there and distract his attention. I don't want him seeing me go past."

"Right-o," she said, and glided through the door and into the lobby.

She dropped the overnight bag in front of the counter, cutting her way into Gustav's conversation, and then apologized profusely for her rudeness. She maneuvered herself between the tiny man and me. I chose a point in the heat of the discussion to slip by.

I ducked into the first elevator and punched the button for the Countess's floor. When the doors opened, I moved quickly down the hall and stopped at the Countess's room, placing my ear against the door. There was a faint sound of activity. Good. The Countess had not yet flown.

I straightened and knocked.

"Yes?"

"Telegram, madam. Very urgent."

The door was unlatched and cautiously opened. The second it had cracked, I slammed into it with all the anger that possessed me. There was a sharp cry as the Countess flew back into the hall, flat on her ass.

I moved in and locked the door behind me, then whirled on her. She was wearing only a robe, and the garment had twisted open, leaving one breast exposed, the hem riding up over her bare hip. She really made a wonderful sight, and if I hadn't been so angry I would have thoroughly enjoyed it.

She saw my look, and adjusted her hem and top with an irritated snap of the garment. "So nice of you to drop in, dear boy. Unexpected company is always a pleasure."

"Let's cut the bullshit," I snapped. "You and I are going to have a little talk, Countess. And if by the time we are through, my government does not have that material neatly sewn up, then I recommend you call your surgeon right now and set up an appointment. Tell him to bring a team. He'll need it if he's ever going to get you put together again.''

She shook her head in exasperation and made a clucking sound with her tongue. ''Nicholas, you really can be quite an ass. Now stop babbling away like a hoodlum and help me up.''

''You can do quite well on your own,'' I growled, ignoring the extended hand.

''Help her up, N3! It's rude to keep a lady waiting!''

I whirled at the sound of the new voice, my mouth dropping open in shock. It was a voice I knew quite well.

There, framed against the sitting room beyond, stood David Hawk, a cigar clamped between his teeth, his body encased in a blue terry cloth robe.

''Carter!'' he snapped. ''The lady, if you don't mind!''

With that he walked off, back into the room.

I finally gathered my wits and lifted the Countess up from the floor. She straightened herself and, with a Cheshire-Cat smile playing over her lips, gestured for me to follow her into the sitting room.

Hawk had wandered over to the terrace doors and was availing himself of the view as we entered. The Countess moved to the drink cabinet and poured me one as I slumped onto the sofa, my mind spinning in a dozen directions at once.

One thing seemed certain. The material was in safe hands, after all. I allowed myself a sigh of relief.

And then I almost burst out laughing. Hawk had chided me on more than a few occasions about my abilities with the ladies. And now, to suddenly find him here, with he and the Countess both in robes, was compromising, to say the least.

A quick look at Hawk showed that he sensed my line of thought. A broad patch of red was spreading across the nape of his neck as he forced his eyes to remain on the view below. Although his face was trying to communicate indifference, the blushing neck was a dead giveaway. I thought it wise not to push my luck by commenting.

It had been obvious in my discussions with him that Hawk had a familiarity with the lady, but I hadn't realized just how far back—or how far, *period*—it had gone. I suddenly understood why I had seen no one covering the lobby. AXE had sent its watchdog, all right. One that could remain very close to the lady. Night *and* day. Hawk had sent Hawk.

A delicate mission, indeed.

The Countess was at my elbow with a drink. "Glad to see you're over your pique." She chuckled. "It really was quite rude, you know."

"Sorry," I said, accepting the drink. "You gave me quite a scare earlier. Forgive me if I was just a bit put out."

She sat down next to me. "You had no reason to be, you know. I was just trying to offer you a little assistance."

I looked at her in disbelief. "And how were you going to do that?"

She flashed me a wide smile and bent her head. Her voice was softly conspiratorial, but the sound was loud enough for all to hear.

"I rather gathered by the surprise on your face at being invited to the auction, not to mention the events themselves, that Theo had rather gotten the best of you so far."

I could feel a tiny patch of red bristling at the back of my own neck.

She gave my arm a patronizing pat as she continued. "You seemed in no danger and in desperate need of an edge, my boy. So I thought I would offer you one. It seemed advantageous to lead him to believe I was double-crossing you. He obviously knew you would be pursuing him, so I thought it might be beneficial to give him a false sense of timing. He might just relax a bit if he thinks you're going to be occupied with me."

I stared at the lady with admiration. "I just wish you would have let me in on it. It definitely would have improved my manners."

Her response was a deep-throated chuckle. "But would it have improved the look of betrayal at the moment you heard me turn?"

I conceded the point. Every agent has to be an actor at some point, and I like to feel I can keep pace with the best. But one does not fool the master so easily. Theo just might have smelled out any dishonest reaction.

I saluted her with my glass. "To you, Countess. And to a performance that had both Theo and me spinning in circles."

She waved the gesture off. "Really, Nicholas. I would have thought you would have caught on. After all, where was I going? We both knew you would have me tailed . . . standard procedure, after all."

I saluted again. "Then to you anyway. A lady who knows her profession."

She laughed heartily. "I was trading state secrets while you were still trading diapers! I am angry with you, however. You could have at least mentioned who it was that you were sending. I hate being unprepared when old friends drop in!"

Her eyes flickered over to Hawk. He rocked a bit on his heels and turned to face her, his mouth clamping more tightly on the butt of his cigar. The patch on his neck brightened to a rosy hue and inched all the way up to his hairline.

But he was spared the necessity of commenting by a knocking at the door.

"That'll be for me," I said. "My cover from MI-6, with Gustav. I asked her to bring him up here."

"Oh?" the Countess said, arching an eyebrow as she rose to answer the door.

"Theo ordered a hit on the hotel we were staying at. Her brother was killed. She's all pro, and she's holding up admirably, but she may need a little of your feminine understanding."

She gave me a reassuring nod before gliding out of the room. Hawk and I could hear her calming Gustav and sending him off, then she reappeared with Belinda.

"We shall leave you two alone. You no doubt have things to discuss." The Countess smiled at us, then turned to the girl beside her. "Come, darling . . . we'll have a discussion of our own." The two moved off into her bedroom.

Hawk had left his position by the window and now moved over to the sofa to join me. "Well," he intoned, "let me have it. Chapter and verse, if you please."

I launched into the whole story—the moves, the manipulations, and finally, the auction and its aftermath. I let it all out, concealing nothing from those sharp eyes and instincts, not even my innermost doubts and self-deprecations.

Hawk listened silently. When I had finished, he rose from the sofa and began pacing the room. "Don't chew yourself up, Nick. Theo is worthy of any opponent. If he weren't, he never would have been hired. You've done your job and done it well. The material will be on its way home. Give yourself credit for that."

"That was only half the assignment," I said. "My job is still to take Theo down, and in view of my performance so far, I'm not one hundred percent sold I can pull it off."

"Theo's tricky," Hawk admitted, "but I've seen you

pull a hell of a lot of magic out of some very small hats."

"You got any spare tricks up your sleeve?"

Hawk sank back into the couch and set his mind to churning. "Well, let's look over the table, shall we? We can't know what cards he's holding, but we do know the man. And we can sure as hell put something together out of the way he's been playing his hands so far. What's the key? What's *motivating* him?"

I moved over to the bar for a refill. "The challenge, I think. He's got a truckload of reasons for everything he's done, but the challenge seems to be what puts the fire in his eyes."

Hawk nodded. "That's the way I make it." And then he snorted. "I just wish I'd seen it earlier."

"How do you mean?" I asked, walking over to one of the chairs and dropping down across from him.

"I should have sensed it; I know the man too well. In the old days we were what you would call hot-rods. Only the most dangerous, most glorious missions would do. The OSS was in its formative years. It needed hot-rods to get on its feet."

"And later?"

He chuckled. "Still plenty of room for ego. With the CIA we got to run around cleaning up the messes. With AXE we got to play empire builders, ultrasecret style. No, there was no shortage of glory there."

"And what about now?"

Hawk stared pensively. "You get older, Nick. The hot-rod just sort of loses its pep and becomes the family car. For me, the transition was a natural one. For Theo, I guess it hurt too much. The vanity just never mellowed. I watched him refusing to get gray on the outside, but I never guessed he was refusing on the inside, too."

"It wouldn't have mattered if you had," I said, shaking my head. "To Theo, AXE is the only challenge left. Even if you'd shelved him, he'd have just come at us from the outside."

Hawk nodded. "No doubt you're right. There is an inevitability to it. The question now is how to take care of it!"

"Year," I said, taking a sip of my drink, "but there's one thing in our favor. The game's narrowed a bit." Hawk gave me a quizzical look. "Before, I had three things to follow up. Now I only have one. The auction's over, and there is no assassin. All I have to concentrate on now is the man himself."

"True," he nodded, smoke curling around his head. "But we have to find him first. Thanks to the lady from MI-6 we've got a channel through Swiss banking, but I'm afraid that'll give Theo too much time to set up."

"I don't think we'll need to use it," I said, digging into my coat pocket. I pulled out the medallion and tossed it on the table in front of Hawk. "I found this on the man who tried to nail me at the hotel. I don't know how to read it, but I'll lay odds it's an engraved invitation."

Hawk picked up the amulet and turned it over slowly in his hands. "Interesting. You're sure it's not just another misdirection? It strikes me as being a little too convenient a clue."

"Ah, but that's just the point," I said, leaning forward intently. "Theo wants the challenge head-to-head. He was adamant about it. And there's no confrontation if I can't find him, is there?"

Hawk gave a thoughtful laugh. "Good old Theo! One thing hasn't changed over the years. With him, there was always one thing you could count on."

"What's that?"

"You couldn't count on anything! That's what made him so brilliant in the field!"

Just then the Countess slipped back into the room.

She edged over to the settee and answered my questioning look with a whisper.

"She's resting."

She then looked from one to the other of us and reacted in typical Countess fashion to our somber expressions.

"Well!" she exclaimed. "Are we going to sit here and brood, or are we going to nail the son-of-a-bitch!"

Hawk looked at her and grinned. "We're gonna get him, all right. The only question is how." Then he reached over and handed her the medallion. "What do you make of this?"

She accepted it and sat herself down next to Hawk to study it.

"The rooster is easy enough," she said. "It's a Portuguese symbol . . . the Barcelos cock. There's a legend about it."

"What is it?" Hawk asked.

"There was a pilgrim traveling through Barcelos who was accused and convicted of theft. He was sentenced to hang but kept insisting on his own innocence. He was finally granted one last appeal and was brought to the home of a judge. The judge was having dinner at the time, one course of which was a platter of roast cock. The pilgrim protested his innocence and claimed, as proof, that the cock would come back to life if he were telling the truth. The pilgrim then prayed to St. James, and sure enough, the miracle occurred to save him."

Hawk's face brightened. "That sounds like Theo. Prayer and miracles."

"What about the thing on the other side, Countess?" I asked. "It's a structure of some sort. Could it be something native to the Barcelos region?"

She gave me a quick look, her instincts, as ever, sharp. "Did Theo give you this?"

"Indirectly, yes. We think it may be a lead."

She studied the second side with greater interest. "Well, I'm not exactly sure what it is, but it does ring a bell. What doesn't feel right is Barcelos. The story occurs there, but the symbol has become universal—all of Portugal has adopted the myth. If there's a key, it lies in whatever this thing on the back is."

"Is there any way we could find out?" I asked.

The Countess rose from the sofa and moved to the corner desk. "The hotel has a guidebook in here. Tourist stuff, mainly. We can browse through it and hope."

Hawk and I looked over her shoulder as she flipped through the pages, our hopes growing slimmer as she neared the end of the book. But then all of a sudden she let out a whoop.

"Gentlemen, I think we may have found it!"

Her manicured finger descended on a page, and Hawk and I moved closer to peer at the photograph.

There was a simple dwelling: low, squat, with a red-tiled peaked roof and fronting terrace. It looked nothing like the structure on the medallion. I was about to comment on that, when my eyes came to rest on the building's chimney. I leaned in and took a closer look. Although not identical to the medallion, the chimney was capped by an odd, very distinctive crown. It was close enough in style to send my hopes soaring. I looked to the top of the page and noted the heading, *The Algarve*, in crisp, neat letters.

"Regional or universal?" I asked, my finger jabbing at the chimney.

The Countess smiled. "Strictly regional. The Algarve is noted for them."

Then it was Hawk's turn. "Algarve . . . Algarve!"

"You got something?" I said.

Hawk nodded, his cigar stabbing out for emphasis. "Ancient history, but it just might be what we're looking for. When the war came to an end, Theo gave heavy

thought to returning to Greece and picking up his life in
the church. I tried to talk him out of it, urging him to return with me and keep his hand in the game. It was a
rough time for him. He was quite torn as to which way to
go, and he said he needed a week away from it all to decide. He told me he needed to be near the ocean—it
helped him to think."

"The Algarve?" I asked.

The Countess jumped in to answer. "It's the south-
ernmost province. It's called the Riviera of Portugal."

"Right!" Hawk nodded. "So I let him go. The last
thing he said before leaving was that God would show
him which way to go. Frankly, on that basis, I never expected to see him again."

"But obviously you did."

"Two days later. He was hitching, and it seems that
the first car to come along was heading his way. The
man dropped him in one of the towns."

Hawk dove for the guidebook and thumbed his way to
the first map he could find. His finger then moved slowly over the southern coastline, finally coming to rest
with a triumphant cry. "Faro! That was it!"

"What made his mind up?"

Hawk discarded the book and began pacing the floor
again. "The man dropped him in the middle of town,
and the first thing Theo did was head for the nearest
church. The front door was locked, so he began circling
the building to find a way in. I guess God was listening
in, because the only door he could find open was one
that led to a side chapel. Theo walked in, took one look
around, and hitched his way back to Lisbon and his new
career."

The Countess lowered her voice to almost a whisper
as she looked at Hawk. "Did he ever tell you what there
was about that chapel that affected him so?"

Hawk nodded slowly. "The chapel was very small but

*very* unusual. It was called the ossuary chapel. Every square inch of wall space was covered with nothing but skulls and bones. Theo took it as the sign he was looking for; somehow he reasoned that God and death could be reconciled."

The Countess screwed up her nose. "A bit morbid, wouldn't you say?"

"Nothing about Theo would surprise me anymore," I groaned. "He went there once for guidance. I think it's a good bet that he's gone back now, don't you, Hawk?"

Hawk lifted the medallion and nodded. "I'm sure of it. Now the only question is how to get at him."

"Yeah," I said. "Theo wrote the book. If I'm going to nail him, I'll have to throw it away. I've got to do the unexpected."

Hawk puffed thoughtfully on his cigar. "Is he vulnerable at any point?"

The memory of his response to Leslie Solari ran quickly through my mind. "Maybe the girl. The minute Kiang put heat in her direction, Theo buckled. He reacted far too quickly and too strongly to be just using her."

Hawk seemed doubtful. "It just doesn't sound like him. Could he maybe have been setting you up . . . another misdirection?"

I considered the possibility, then rejected it. "No. Kiang's appearance was unanticipated. The reaction came from his guts; of that I'm certain."

"Remember, David," the Countess said, "we're not talking about a mission here. He's got his haul, and he's looking to retire. One might keep involvements out of one's career, but you could get pretty lonely trying to spend a quarter of a billion dollars by yourself. Especially when you can't very well spread it around openly."

"Good point, Countess," Hawk said, nodding at her, and then he turned to me. "Speaking of girls, what are you going to do with your lady friend from MI-6?"

"I think it would be best if we sent her home," I said.

From across the room came an adamant reply. "No!"

I looked up to see Belinda standing in the doorway to the bedroom.

"I've been assigned to this bloody mission," she said, stepping defiantly up to us, "and I'll not have myself relieved on account of pity. I've got a stake in this now, and I fully intend to see it through."

"But, Belinda, you have no—"

"Forgive me," she interrupted, "but I've been listening in. I think you're going to need an edge, Nick, and you've got one with me. Your man thinks I'm dead. We know I'm not. He's going to be looking for you to come at him alone. Perhaps we can disappoint him."

"She's got a point," Hawk growled. "On the one hand, Theo thinks you'll be tied up with the Countess for a while, so you've got speed working for you. On the other, he won't be expecting you to arrive with assistance. It could work to your advantage."

I turned back to Belinda. "This man is a master agent, luv. He's ruthless and—"

"I'm very well aware of that," she replied, her voice like ice. "But I do have one request."

"Which is . . . ?"

"This is a field termination, correct? For both parties?"

I nodded.

"And it's your opinion the connection between them is a strong one?"

Again I nodded.

"Then I want the girl. At some point and in some manner so that he can watch her die. That's all I ask."

Her voice was chilling in its resolve.

"Okay," I replied. "We go . . . first thing in the morning."

# THIRTEEN

The Algarve takes its name from the Arabic *El-Gharb*, meaning the West. It was the farmost western conquest of the ancient Moors, and the pervading atmosphere of the province takes its flavor more from Mediterranean Africa than the Portuguese influences of the north.

It's the playground of millions, with centrally located Faro as its capitol and hub. Tourists pile in for the low rates, either moving east for the sandy, flat beaches, or west for the high-cliffed inlets and coves.

The Riviera of Portugal.

From where I stood the mood was anything but playful. We had found Theo's church, the Igreja do Carmo, a Carmelite sanctuary tucked quietly near the Faro city center. From the outside it appeared like any other edifice, with its twin baroque towers and faded, simple facade.

One could almost ignore it, sitting in the open square that fronted it and sipping one's *cerveja*, without ever knowing the uniqueness concealed by the surrounding walls. But for the curious, a quick walk through the tall iron gate leading to the south transept would reveal a sight both eerie and awesome.

160

The chapel of bones. Theo's private inspiration.

That is where I now stood.

I placed myself in the chapel's center, my left and right flanked by tiny pews for the faithful. But my eyes refused to leave the walls. Every direction I turned, I was faced with skulls and bones, their bleached whiteness radiating an inner brightness that seemed to illuminate the darkened chapel with deathly light.

On first contact, the question had planted itself in my brain. What kind of man would find an answer in a setting such as this?

But later, as I stood and absorbed the atmosphere, the question seemed as mute as the walls themselves. One had only to think of Theo, the religious disciple turned death merchant. Then I understood the impact this sight must have made on the young shepherd priest. The chapel was a monument to the contradictory forces of death and afterlife.

It was Theo, in stone and bone.

With this realization came an ironic surge of optimism. In the aftermath of the events in Lisbon, staking out the chapel had seemed only the longest of long shots. But now, as I actually stood experiencing the room, the gamble seemed far more of a reality than before.

None of us had felt this kind of certainty in the tense atmosphere of Lisbon. Not the Countess, nor Hawk, nor Belinda . . . least of all myself. We had arisen after the chaos of Saturday intent on devising our strategy. While the city filled up its churches, sunlight filled up the Ritz suite. While the natives sang their praises to eternal life, we contemplated calculated death.

Our options were few and limited, but between Hawk and myself we were able to piece together some kind of analysis of the man and his methods. It was an outline, at best. Theo was beyond definitions. He was just too smart. We could only hope we would be smarter.

One thing we felt certain about was that Theo already had his hole picked out. The money he had made selling out AXE was enough to buy him a sanctuary and secure it to some degree. The auction money would enable him to make it a fortress.

Even now, going directly at him would have to be difficult. Later it would be next to impossible. That is, if we could even find him. He had given us his clue—the Algarve—but that occupied some six hundred square kilometers of territory, and the man could be anywhere within that area.

Belinda offered the services of MI-6—and their intimate relations with the Portuguese authorities—to try and locate the couple, but Hawk and I put it on hold. Manhunts, no matter how well orchestrated, are loud and noisy affairs. Too many questions get asked; too many arms get twisted. By the time any real information is gained, the target knows more about your progress than you do. He can bar the gate, or flee.

Assuming we could locate him, the only way we were going to get Theo was to draw him out, pull him from the safety of his nest. But this too had its drawbacks. Theo knew he was hunted. He would be wary of anything that seemed to call him from his safety.

The Countess suggested that Leslie Solari might be an approach. She would be easier to lure, and if the connection between the two defectors was an intimate one, Theo might just have to move out to save her. But once more, Hawk and I dismissed it. If the girl was the chink in Theo's armor, he would take great pains to keep that breach well away from the enemy's reach.

The only thing that got unanimous agreement was that if Theo was going to be drawn out, it would have to be within the next week. The Countess had planted her ruse at the auction. To Theo, she was the double-crosser, and I would be locked in trying to correct the damage.

It was just possible that for a few days his guard would be down. He might let himself get careless. But at the end of that week the first payment would come due at the first bank, and Theo would know the issue had been resolved. The game would be on for real. Delaying payment would only arouse his suspicions; making it would only buy him the cover and protection he needed to set up.

It was this first week or not at all.

The only starting point we had was the ossuary chapel in Faro. It was a place of significance for him, and it was likely he would touch base there. Feeling secure, he just might use his first few days for the luxury of recreation. If he did, it might be in the form of a final farewell before wrapping himself in his cocoon.

The church was the key.

The question was how to maintain a constant surveillance without arousing undue curiosity or suspicion. I couldn't very well stand around in the open all week, waiting for Theo to show.

A simple guidebook gave me the answer.

It was a Carmelite church, made up of both friars and nuns.

Father O'Hanlon hadn't worked too well before. Maybe this time the cover would.

I pitched the idea to Hawk and Belinda.

"MI-6 contacts the church hierarchy for permission. Belinda and I don collar and habit and fly in. We take up our duties as acolytes and wait."

Belinda thought it just might work.

Hawk hit the roof.

"It won't work. He knows the cover—he's seen you!"

"Wrong," I argued. "He saw photos of the setup at the bar, and he saw *me* at the auction. The closest he ever got to the good Father was probably a description from Martinez. And how many priests are there in this world that fit that description? He can't check them all out."

Hawk still seemed uncertain as I pushed the point further.

"Besides, he'd never suspect I'd use the same cover twice. And even if he does give it a second thought, I'm not walking in alone. Belinda and I will arrive at the airport at Faro together. A priest and a nun—assistance he thinks he got rid of back at the Lisboa Plaza. The *unexpected*, Hawk!"

Hawk was still doubtful but weakening. "Okay, but what about inside the chapel? He'd spot you for sure."

"Let's hope so," I said grimly. "By then we're face-to-face, and he's all but dead."

Hawk finally bit. "It's risky . . . downright insane." Then a smile broke across his face, and his cigar poked in my direction. "And that's exactly why it may work! You've got one week—just until the first payment hits the bank. If he doesn't show by then, we pull out and go into backup. Agreed?"

"Agreed!"

We broke the meeting around one o'clock, with Hawk and the Countess using their own muscle to persuade MI-6, the church, and the Portuguese. Sunday night found a priest and a nun winging their way into Faro, and Monday learning the layout and regimen of the Carmelite order.

By Tuesday morning we were part of the chapel routine; Belinda in the light, I among the bones in the shadows.

The gamble was on.

"Nick . . . ?"

I turned as Belinda stepped into the chapel through the heavy oaken door that led from the courtyard.

"Over here," I hissed around the edge of the heavy cowl.

She moved quickly toward me, the swishing sound of her heavy habit echoing in the chamber.

"What's up?" I whispered.

"Trouble . . . I think."

"How so?"

"We've got a couple of lovebirds in one hell of a hurry to tie the knot."

"So?" I didn't get her concern. Marrying in Portugal was a fairly regular thing, even on the spur of the moment. "That's what priests and chapels are for."

"Nick . . . our lovebirds are pushing seventy."

Outside, the tower chimes began to count out the hour of seven. In the back of my mind, a second set of bells began to ring faintly.

"Pregnancy's out. Why the hurry?" I asked, following Belinda toward the front of the chapel.

"Seems the lady has cancer. She's been a maiden all her life, by the look of it. But it appears as though she found herself someone to give her a final fling. Rather a well-preserved chap for his age, I'd say. At any rate, she's hot to have it done and insists on tonight. The really odd touch is that she wants it done in here."

"Hmmm, very interesting," I murmured.

"Don't get your hopes up, luv," Belinda smiled, seating herself in the first pew. "They're a ways off from our two. She's a Frenchy . . . very pale and gray-haired. He's a local, also gray-headed, with a mustache as thick as your fist."

I sat down beside her in the pew. "Who's doing the

talking? Who's the one pushing for the chapel?"

"The woman," she answered. "She's plotting it all out with Father Barrault. I suspect that half the reason she's speaking French is to keep her beau from hearing the details. He seems terrified of the whole idea."

"Damn," I muttered, leaning back in the pew, feeling my excitement ebb.

Belinda reached over and patted my hand. "Sorry. Maybe the next pair."

There was a faint click of heels at the back of the chapel that brought both of us up in our seats. Hands were quickly separated, bodies thrust into prayerful positions. Belinda turned briefly to eye the newcomer. Then she turned back, her smile impish, her voice a faint breath of a whisper.

"It's the beau. He's checking out the show. I give him two minutes, and the wedding's off."

I hushed her into silence and turned to study the unsuspecting groom. His head was turned away slightly, his eyes absorbing the sight surrounding him. I studied the profile, admiring the good looks behind the silver-gray hair and mustache. Whatever fears Belinda had sensed in the man regarding the chapel seemed to have fled with the actual encounter.

There was awe in his expression . . . total, reverent awe.

Suddenly there was terror in mine. The bells were back in force.

I turned back so quickly that Belinda jumped. She opened her mouth to question my reaction, but I stilled the query with a quick grip of her hand. There was a brief wince, then growing understanding as she felt the chill bite of my fingers into her flesh.

"My God!" she breathed.

He was twenty feet away, and I could taste him. At

the moment I was weaponless. The chapel didn't open to the public for another two hours, and my weaponry was sitting back in the cell I'd been assigned as home for the week. *This* trip to the chapel proper had been for my benefit.

That didn't mean I couldn't kill him, of course. I'd almost relish the feel of his throat in my hands. But I didn't know if he was armed. And twenty feet might just as well be twenty miles with someone of Theo's caliber. Could I risk it? Could I make it to him before he saw through my disguise?

Not likely. Wasn't I seeing through his?

In my mind I gave him a point. The mustache was fake, a good one but fake nonetheless. The hair wasn't. Theo had always been scrupulous about keeping the approaching gray out of his hair with chemicals . . . until now.

Could I reach him?

I doubted it, and Belinda sensed it.

"You'll never make it, Nick," she whispered. "The distance is too far."

"I know. Get him out! We'll have to try later."

Her hand eased up on mine, and her body lifted quickly from the pew. She gave a clipped genuflect and sped off toward the man at the rear of the chapel. I listened to each footfall, counting the closing gap, wishing the steps were mine. Then I leaned forward, my hands clasping in the attitude of prayer, my ears turning back to listen for the sound of his voice.

It was Belinda who spoke first, her voice remarkably even, her accent thickly Italian. *Compreendo mal o Português. Fala Italiano . . . fala Inglês?"*

*"Sim,"* Theo answered, his own accent thickly Portuguese. "I speak . . . uh . . . little English."

"We are closed now," Belinda informed him. "The

chapel is open later. Come later, yes?"

I could feel the burning concentration of the man's eyes on my back. "A priest," Theo murmured. "He is of your order, yes?"

"Yes," Belinda replied. "He prays." There was a hesitant pause. "He prays for the death of a friend."

I felt the eyes lift from my body. There was a second more of silence, and then a voice contrived in its awkwardness. "I am to marry. Tonight. Here I will marry."

Belinda responded with appropriate joy. "An event both blessed, and joyously awaited by us. But now, you must be gone. Father Barrault will arrange you. Until tonight. Go with God, *senhor*. Go with God."

I waited until the door closed firmly behind them before unlocking my body and easing myself back onto the hard surface of the pew.

The gamble had paid off . . . in spades. Theo *was* serious about Leslie Solari. He would marry her, then let himself go gray, burying them in anonymity beneath the fruits of his labors.

Well, at least he could try.

# FOURTEEN

There was a stiff breeze whipping across the darkened plaza. It climbed the outside perimeter walls of the chapel and twisted through the courtyard, biting at the hem of my robe. Its source was the harbor several blocks away, and it carried with it the stench common to waterfronts the world over.

From the front of the church came the sudden tolling of the bells. It mingled with the wind to give the scene a macabre atmosphere. I peered up at the source. The bell tower stood framed against a starry sky, the moon hanging just to its left. It was almost full, giving it a skull-like appearance that would have rivaled any in the decor of the chapel behind me.

Eleven o'clock.

I heard steps treading toward the gate and pushed myself back into the entry of the chapel. My body eased somewhat at the sight of Belinda moving through the gate. She crossed the courtyard and climbed the steps, fighting the breeze as it tore at her habit.

"They should be here any second. You're watching for the car?"

I nodded.

"Anxious?" Her eyes were sympathetic and warm.

I peered off down the street. In the distant wash of light two drunks stepped from a bar. "Yeah."

Her hand came up to lightly touch my chest. "But ready."

I turned back and smiled. "Ready as hell."

She reached down and pulled something from her waistband. "Here," she said, slipping the object over my head. "A good luck piece."

I stared down. Hanging on the end of a gold chain was the medallion that had led us to where we now stood. "So this is where you disappeared to this afternoon," I chuckled, then looked into her lovely, sparkling eyes. "Thanks . . . a lot."

I received a quick peck on the lips. "Well, the wedding was arranged, and I didn't have any reason for mucking about here. Did a little touring, I did. Got me a charm, too."

She reached for her chest and held out a large silver cross.

"I didn't know you were religious," I teased.

"Not usually," she blushed. "But I kind of feel as though we're on Theo's territory . . . the chapel and all. Just want to feel like God is not entirely on his side." She let the amulet fall back to rest against her body.

Involuntarily my hand drifted over to my forearm. Hugo was in place, nestled in his sheath. I then checked my waistband. Wilhelmina sat in place, her silencer pressing against the upper reaches of my thigh.

"Well," I said, "if God's not, we've got a few other friends who are. You did bring your pistol, I trust?"

"No." I stared at her. "Just a precaution. We know we've got him the second he enters that chapel. I didn't want him accidentally bumping into me and finding something that would scare him off. Just playing it safe."

Her words made sense, but I nodded reluctantly. "Be careful."

"You too, Nick," she whispered, pressing her body closer to mine.

Checking the area quickly, I pulled her into me and lowered my lips to hers. It was a long kiss, both encouraging and exciting. It was broken by the sound of a car engine.

"I think we've got company," I growled, both of us moving deeper into the shadows.

The car drifted up the square and swung against the curb across from us. Two bodies emerged into the overhead glow of the streetlamp. The light bounced off twin silver heads.

The blood in my body began to pump.

"Go get 'em," I said, giving Belinda a pat on her rump.

"With pleasure," she answered, and marched her way down the steps as I retreated back into the chapel.

I moved quickly down the aisle, stepped up onto the dais that fronted the altar, and turned to give the room a final sweep.

There was a windless, eerie silence in the chapel. In the flickering candlelight, the skulls on the wall seemed to be smiling. Twisted, ossified grins . . . as if they knew what was coming.

At the sound of approaching footsteps, I turned my back on the aisle and knelt before the altar. Wilhelmina crept from my belt and nestled into my palm. My head dropped in prayer, and I clasped my hands before me. Wilhelmina felt hard, cold . . . and deadly.

The door at the end of the chapel groaned open, and I could hear Belinda soothing our guests into the trap. The words were lost to me, but not the identities. There was Theo's confident bass, mingling with Leslie's gentle alto, both being coaxed to the front by Belinda.

The sounds stilled as the footsteps halted behind me.

For a moment longer I held myself in prayerlike repose, my finger curling over the trigger, Wilhelmina settling into my palm until she was no longer something apart. Both Luger and silencer were an extension of my arm.

"Father?" came the tentative plea. It was Leslie in accented French. "We are ready, Father."

I lifted my body from the floor, rising to full height, and then slowly turned to them, moving the gun behind me as I did.

My eyes lit first on the woman, then flickered over to Theo.

He was smiling, but it quickly faded to a puzzled frown. The years had honed his instincts to a fine turn, and now they were working full bore.

His brows creased as his eyes began to move until they found the Algarve medallion around my neck. His brow furrowed, and then his eyes saucered open in realization.

The girl meant to scream as I brought Wilhelmina up, but it came out a choked gasp.

"Don't try it, Theo."

My words caught the man, his hand jerking toward his coat. His hand fell back, but his mind was obviously cranking out the possibilities. I could almost hear the wheels turning. *He hasn't shot me yet. Until he does, there's hope. Engage him in chatter, and wait for an opening.*

"So, Nick," he smiled. "It seems you've moved a bit faster, and a bit more accurately, than I anticipated."

My answer was a clipped command to Belinda. "Frisk them."

Belinda checked Theo. She removed the gun from inside his coat, then assured me with her nod that it was all he possessed. She then followed suit with the girl.

Leslie was clean; she was also shaking with fright.

Theo stared at Belinda, his mind once more trying to piece together some kind of understanding. "Not alone, I see," he hissed, then his head jerked back to me. "You disappoint me, Nick."

"How is that, Theo?" I growled.

"I thought you would accept my challenge in the manner it was offered. I gave you proof of my sincerity. I warned you of the attempt on your friends. I'm sorry you didn't reach them in time, but I did try to save them. I thought you'd honor our agreement, meet me man-to-man, but instead you find yourself another ally."

My voice came out flat and cold. "No, Theo, no new allies. The same ally as before. Only her brother didn't make it. Your killers wasted the wrong girl."

Theo turned to look at Belinda. The look he received in return chilled even my blood. Theo watched as Belinda's eyes drifted from him and settled onto Leslie, who began to shuffle her feet nervously. Theo had a clear understanding of what the look implied. His body stiffened, and his mind went into overdrive.

He turned back to me. When he spoke, his voice was as flat and cold as mine had been.

"Where are your guts, Nick? Man-to-man . . . what do you say?"

I paused before answering, flicking a glance at Belinda. "Don't know, Theo. The lady has a stake in this. It was her brother."

Theo's answering smile was full of sarcasm. "I can hardly fight man-to-man with a woman, Nick. But I'm willing . . . after I've finished with you."

"There's no need," Belinda said.

Three loud blasts cut the stillness of the chapel. There was a scream after the first shot only. The second shot carried Leslie back into the aisle, and the third slammed her up against the back of the first pew.

Theo watched horrified as she slumped slowly down and then slammed to the floor. There was the faintest of moans, then the final sigh that signified death.

"Jesus, you're a cold-blooded bitch!" Theo roared, his composure completely broken.

"No more than you're a cold-blooded bastard," Belinda replied evenly, and turned to me. "I'm square with him . . . now it's your turn."

Out of the corner of my eye I watched Theo move to Leslie's body. My first instinct was to blow him away right then and get it over with.

I should have followed that instinct.

It was very touching the way he stooped to cradle her lifeless form, his fingers combing through the hair on the lolling head.

It hit me, but a second too late. Theo wasn't caressing the dead woman's hair; he was searching through it.

Leslie's body crashed to the floor as Theo leaped up from behind the pew. With the barest flick of his wrist, he sent a small spherical object hurling straight in my direction. The dim light of the room played off the object, caressing it, and screaming out recognition.

Pierre!

It was not *my* Pierre, of course. I had left my own tiny, round gas bomb in my cell. But AXE issued the lethal objects to all its agents. Obviously Theo had taken some with him on his departure and—ever the prepared spy— had planted one on his lady friend, but Belinda had missed it in the search. It wasn't her fault; that's what they were designed for.

The problem now was to avoid the deadly results.

"Duck!" I screamed, throwing myself off to the right, working against the angle of flight. I could only hope that Belinda would respond on instinct. She couldn't know what it was she was avoiding.

I hit the edge of the dais and rolled down the few steps to the chapel floor. I gave a quick look behind, trying to determine the flow of the vapors. There were none. What I saw instead brought a curse to my lips.

The object had hit the altar with a click and bounced harmlessly to the floor. As it did, I was able to make out what it really was . . . not a deadly gas bomb, but one of the large pearl spheres that had topped Leslie's handbag.

Chalk up one for the teacher.

How many hours had we spent as rookies learning to counter our own equipment? How many times had I stood in Training and Development dodging the very pellets that had so effectively worked against the enemy? And Theo knew it. He had usually done the tossing.

A conditioned response. The man, the object—and I had reacted like one of Pavlov's dogs to the stimulus.

I fired too quick rounds into the area where Theo had been, hoping against hope that Belinda had *failed* to respond to my command. I rolled and rose up in a crouched position.

Too late. She had apparently heeded my warning. What was also apparent was that Theo had used the dodge to come up behind her.

He now had her by the throat, his huge forearms crushing into her windpipe, his other hand pulling the gun from her grasp. No sooner did he see me rise, than he swung the girl between us, using her as a shield to keep me from firing.

Before I could shift over for a better angle, he began dragging her back up the aisle. As he did, he let off one quick shot, firing into the air, to let me know he had control of the weapon. I froze and trained Wilhelmina on him, hoping for one clean shot before he could make the door.

Belinda's eyes bulged, partly from trying to gasp for air, partly from an apparent fear that I might be willing to shoot them both rather than let Theo make it to freedom.

And I might have, but Belinda solved the dilemma.

Her hands had been groping for the silver cross hanging at her hip as Theo tugged her along. Just as they reached the door, she got it.

When Theo leaned back and turned slightly to open the heavy door, Belinda quit fighting. In turn, his grip on her relaxed just enough so that she could bring the cross up directly into the side of his neck.

While not sharp enough to pierce the skin, it raised hell with the side of his windpipe.

He gagged and staggered backward, releasing Belinda. She fell like a stone and rolled between the last two pews.

Theo got one shot off at her, and I fired once at him as he hurled himself through the door.

I knew I missed, and since there was no sound from Belinda, I figured he had as well.

I rushed up the aisle to where I had seen her go down. "Belinda . . . ?"

There was no reply, and I quickly saw why. A welt had already risen on her right temple. Blood from the gash was minimal, but she was out cold.

I guessed that her head had collided with the edge of the pew on the way down.

She was alive, and that's what mattered.

And so was Theo.

I was rising and inching my way toward the door when the loud cranking of an engine broke the air. The car!

Bursting through the open door, I leaped down the chapel steps, raced across the courtyard and tossed myself through the gate. I hit the cobbled street and rolled to a kneeling position just as the car sped away from the curb. There was no sign of anyone behind the wheel. But then, there wouldn't be. He would be crouched across the seat, waiting until he had gained some distance before he would risk exposing himself.

I lowered Wilhelmina and blasted out four shots.

Two tires blew, sending the car into a screeching skid that arched it toward the stone wall to my left. In spite of the ruptured tires, the car kept coming, angling relentlessly toward the brickwork.

I was out of the path, so I stretched myself out flat on my stomach, my eyes riveted on the ground beyond the automobile, waiting for the barest hint of his body tossing itself from the car.

None came.

Not even after the car slammed into the wall.

The night air was filled with the sound of grinding metal and shattering glass. In the midst of the collision, the driver's door flew open, and a large paving stone dropped out onto the sidewalk. As it did, the engine ceased its grinding roar and settled into the calmer sounds of idling.

Reality hit home with a vengeance.

There never had been anyone inside. Theo had only to crank up the engine, lever the accelerator with the brick, slip over to the passenger door, and pop the car in gear the moment I showed. My focus would be on the vehicle, and as I rolled to the street, so would he.

That would put Theo's present position somewhere across the way.

I was a sitting duck.

As if in answer to my thoughts, two loud cracks drifted out on the wind. There was a dull flash of sparks about one foot away from my face as the bullets struck against the cobblestones. I rolled back toward the curb and readied to return fire. But there was no need.

Instead of further gunfire, there came only a resonant

laugh and a shouted taunt.

"That's one, Nick. One chance I had to kill you. Too easy, though. No challenge in that one. But one more is all you get. One more reprieve, Nick. The third time you're mine!"

Now I knew it . . . the man had gone over the deep end. Theo was nuts.

At the final word, he bolted. There was only the briefest flash of his broad back as he rounded the nearest corner and ran. There wasn't even time for me to take aim.

I leaped to my feet and ran in the direction of the departing footsteps. As I went, I popped the clip from Wilhelmina's butt, then reached into my waistband and brought out a new one, slamming it home as I raced to the corner. It was standard procedure to count rounds. I had fired three in the chapel and four outside. *If* Theo was counting, I wanted to be able to produce more than anticipated. It was slim, but it was still a chance to gain the upper hand.

And I needed every advantage, dealing with a madman.

A lot of things made a lot of sense now. Theo had cracked, but he couldn't give up. He couldn't kill himself, and he couldn't give up the game.

So I was to be his executioner, or be executed myself and become the final unction to cleanse his soul.

I hit the corner and peered cautiously around its edge. I was on the apex end of a triangular-shaped block. That left the man two ways to go. Either he was dead ahead of me, or he had turned the second corner and worked his way up the angled block. There was no way I could move over to check out the angle without exposing myself to fire from the street ahead.

I stiffened my body and listened. There were no sounds of feet, only the constant whistle of the wind. If he was dead ahead, he was stationed at no greater distance than what I had just traveled myself. If he was up the angled block, he could conceivably be walking, backing his way slowly up the block, hoping that the breeze would muffle the sound.

I would have to gamble, but which way? Hawk's words drifted through my brain. *With Theo there was always one thing you could count on: you couldn't count on anything!* It wasn't a comforting thought, but it did offer one grain of hope.

When you've been in the field as long as I have, even the unexpected becomes somewhat predictable. Any agent who is well trained and has years of experience under his belt has learned to reduce himself to one single denominator in a time of stress.

Instinct.

It's the primal link with survival.

Theo was on the run, all senses keyed to survival. What had been *his* instinct when he had rounded this corner moments before?

He had faced an open street on the one hand, an angled one on the other. The open street gave him nothing but a showdown. The angled one offered exactly what he needed.

Time.

He was up the angled corner, no doubt about it. The question now was what he would do with his time. He would not escape. He would never give up his long-awaited battle.

I stepped out and moved to the other blunted edge of the apex. I looked up the street. It was dark and quiet, a few cars parked on either side, with the only light coming from the open front of a neighborhood bar.

I stared farther up the street. The block was too long for Theo to have made the other corner. There just hadn't been enough time. He was either holed up along the street, or he had entered the bar.

I crouched and then soundlessly rolled from the curb until I was under the front bumper of the first car. I sighted down Wilhelmina's barrel through the long tunnel of undercarriages.

No one . . . nothing.

Rolling over the cobbled street, I repeated the process with the second line of cars.

Again, nothing but the grimy underside of machinery.

Cautiously I rose and moved from car to car. It wasn't long until I had a clear shot of the whole street, both sides.

Now I had confirmation. Theo was inside the bar. All the buildings on the street were flat-faced, in the old European style of using every square foot for living. The doors opened directly onto the curb.

An old dictum of Theo's suddenly hit me, bringing a smile to my face.

*When you're stalking, Nick, use the old myth of the woman who would be married, but the man thinks she could not care less. Surely you've heard it, Nick. A man chases a woman until she catches him! Do the same with your prey, Nick. Let him chase you until you've got him! Let him get closer and closer, until suddenly you're behind him. Then, let him run for a while!*

The bastard planned on letting me move on by the bar and then doubling in behind me.

I moved toward the bar and scanned the interior through a corner of the front window.

The room was moderately full; locals out for an evening brew. It was also sparsely furnished, a bare, open structure that offered no hiding. There was no sign of Theo, but then I didn't think there would be. The scenario was very clear in my mind. It was time to play out my part.

I parked Wilhelmina and moved.

When I entered, my priestly garments brought a hush to the room. I ignored the stares and moved straight to the bartender. I quickly described Theo and asked if he had been in. The bartender confirmed that he had, in a great hurry, stopping only long enough to inquire about the bar's rear exit.

I smiled, thanked the man, and followed his directions to the back of the house, moving to the rear of the room and through a pair of dark curtains that led into a hall containing the rest room and the rear exit. The clamor resumed behind me as I moved past the washroom doors and threw open the door to the alleyway beyond.

I waited a beat or two, and then slammed the door shut, leaving myself inside in the process. I then moved quietly back through the curtains. By peering around the edge of the curtains, I had a direct view into the short hall. I concentrated on the door to the washroom.

There was a space of a minute or two before the door inched its way open. Theo's head appeared, and I released my hold on the cloth, filling my hand with Wilhelmina. I counted beats and footsteps, then thrust myself back into the hall. I caught Theo with his hand on the door.

The man turned, recognition draining the color from his face. I lifted my gun, taking dead aim on his forehead, but fate chose that moment to burst open the door from the toilet a second time. A man lurched out, intent only on weaving his way back to his drinking buddies.

As he did, the door slammed into my wrist, sending Wilhelmina's shot slamming harmlessly into the stucco of the upper wall, and Wilhelmina herself skittering onto the floor. The drunk took one look at me, one look at the gun on the floor, and dived back into the john.

Theo had his own gun out, the barrel on its way toward my head.

"This is only number two, Theo," I hissed. "What happened to the game?"

He shrugged. "It's gone too far. Believe me, Nick, I was almost hoping you would win."

The curtains behind Theo parted. Just as he fired, three Portuguese fishermen shoved through, cursing and gesturing.

I rolled to the side.

The slug hit the wall inches from my head, spraying plaster like a fine mist throughout the tiny passageway.

In the chaos, the three fishermen tripped over each other trying to back off. Theo's escape that way was blocked. He lunged toward the rear door behind me, but not before I got a shoulder in his gut.

The blow was solid but not strong enough to put him down. His momentum shattered the door from its hinges, and Theo was on his knees in the alley.

I groped and found Wilhelmina. By the time I brought her into action, there was no more Theo.

I rolled into the alley with Wilhelmina ready. Theo was just rounding the corner at the alley's end. There was no time to get off a round before he was gone.

And then it hit me. There *had* been time for Theo to get off another shot when he was crouched in the alley and I was groping for my Luger.

Why hadn't he?

And then I remembered the slack-jawed grin he had flashed just before I'd dived to avoid his first shot.

Had he really missed because he had been distracted by the three fishermen?

Or was his crazy little game still on!

I started to trot up the alley after him, then stopped. Chasing him was suddenly pointless.

I knew where he was going.

# FIFTEEN

I entered the chapel and closed the doors behind me. Belinda was still lying where I had left her. I checked her breathing and pulse. Both were at a reassuring level of normality.

Lifting her gently, I carried her up to the front of the chapel. I settled her down in the front pew, hoping that when the gunplay started, the thick wood would offer some protection.

As I stretched her out over the seat, her eyes fluttered open, a distant moan spilling from her chest.

"Is he dead?" she whispered, her words slightly slurred, her eyes still struggling to focus.

"No," I answered, stroking her hair. "He ran. I followed. He had a shot at me, but he didn't use it. At least I don't think he did."

"What does that mean?" she asked, gingerly rubbing the now purpled bump on her pretty head.

"I don't know . . . yet."

"Where is he now?"

"Running . . . somewhere."

"Why aren't you after him?"

"No need. He'll run for a while, and then he'll come here."

She eyed me uncertainly. "How can you be sure? What if he doesn't?"

I smiled. "He will, luv. I know it."

She either accepted my certainty or was still too dazed to argue, but she gave a light nod. Then her brow furrowed with concern.

"You had a chance, Nick. While he was backing off with me. You could have taken him then, but you didn't." Her eyes looked intently into mine. "It was me, wasn't it? You let him go because of me?"

My hand gently traced the line of her chin. "I considered it, Belinda. I almost fired the gun in spite of you."

"But you didn't have to, because I used the cross?"

I shrugged, averting my eyes.

"Hey, bastard," she said after a moment.

"What?"

"I'm talking to you."

"I'm listening."

"But you're not talking back." Her hand found my chin and swiveled my eyes back to hers.

"What if I hadn't had the cross? . . . If I hadn't used it?"

"We'll never know, will we?" I attempted a feeble smile. "You're lucky you got him right in the windpipe. Otherwise—"

"I didn't."

"Huh?"

"I didn't get him right in the windpipe. I barely grazed his throat, but it was enough."

"I don't get it."

She shoved the cross into my hand. "Hold the base against your palm."

I did. "So?"

She waited until it was firmly in place, and then she reached inside her habit. She withdrew a small metal box, no bigger than a matchbook. On one face of it was a small, pressure-sensitive heat cell. She gave the plate the briefest touch, and a jolt of electricity leaped from the cross, traveling up my arm like a train.

For a second my muscles contracted, and then they rebelled, tossing the object from my grasp.

Belinda chuckled and pulled the cross from around her neck, tossing it to me.

"Just another precaution, luv," she said. "I know we had the drop on him, but your man is a bright one. So I spent the day preparing in case we had to move in hand-to-hand. I wanted to have a little surprise ready!"

I stared at the amulet in my hand and then into her twinkling eyes. "Now who's the bastard!" I said, chuckling myself.

A cloud passed over her eyes, erasing the levity of a moment before. When she spoke it was through lips set in a taut line.

"Theo is, and he's still alive."

"Yeah," I nodded. "I'm about to work on that."

Suddenly her eyes jumped and her head lolled. At the same time all life seemed to leave her body. I leaned forward and touched her, but her response was lifeless.

"Belinda . . ."

And then a faint sound hit me from behind.

It came from the area where the chapel concealed its connecting door with the church proper. Company had arrived, and judging from Belinda's quick and clever retreat into unconsciousness, it was no secret just who the company was.

Theo had returned to the womb.

I started to rise, but the voice from behind halted me.

"Slowly, Nick. Get up very slowly and very carefully."

I obeyed, showing the man my outstretched hands.

"Welcome home, Theo."

"Toss the gun away," he ordered. "Throw it back into the pews. Make it travel. The knife, too. Slowly, Nick!"

I tossed Wilhelmina and watched as she clattered between the rows, coming to rest about three quarters of the way toward the back of the chapel. I then withdrew Hugo from his sheath. At the same time, I opened my right hand, letting the cross dangle down, its chain woven between my fingers.

Hugo then joined Wilhelmina.

"Turn," came the voice.

I did, turning slowly in place, my head revolving to take in the man's face. His expression said he smelled victory. His eyes burned with anticipation, and his smile was tight and anxious.

"Thought you might come back."

"I guess you did," he snapped. "But you obviously didn't expect me to use the back door. Careless of you, Nick. I've spent my life around churches. There's never only one entry to any part. You should have anticipated that. After all, you're the one who's been living here."

"Yeah, I suppose I should have anticipated it," I growled. "Stupid of me, wasn't it?"

I lifted the cross and began staring at it. I looked back at Theo and held it out to him. I moved toward him, taking each step he would give me as he studied my offering. Finally came the words I was expecting.

"Hold it, Nick. You're close enough."

I stopped, lowering my hand to toss the cross. Every motion was handled slowly. I didn't want to spook the man into firing. "Here, Theo. To the winner. A symbol for your victory." Carefully, I tossed it to him, hoping he wouldn't notice it was the same cross that had given him such a hell of a jolt before.

He caught it and weighed it in his fingers, never taking his eyes from me. I continued talking as he stared back.

"It's over, Theo. I'm tired of the game, and I think you are too. You killed the others. Now it's my turn."

"Like I said before, Nick, it's a pity in a lot of ways. You see, I win both ways."

"I know, Theo. I think I figured it out. You don't have the guts to do it yourself, do you? Or, maybe even more important, it's against your religion to do it yourself. So you set me up as your executioner. But even that wasn't enough. You couldn't just let me kill you. That would have bruised your already bruised ego too much."

"You through?"

"Not quite. If I did miss, you would have proved to yourself that you were still the best. That would have allowed you to live with yourself. You want to know what I think, Theo?"

"I'm listening . . . for about ten more seconds."

"I think you're nuts, Theo . . . bonkers, whacko, around the bend. I think you're rowing with only one oar in the water."

A bright red flush spread across his face, and the hand holding the cross squeezed into a fist.

I waited until I was sure the base of the cross was solid against his palm.

"Belinda!"

Belinda came in right on cue. Theo's eyes grew huge in their sockets, and his gun arm twisted up spastically from the jolt. As muscles contracted, his finger clamped down on the trigger, sending a loud burst into the air that loosened one of the bones in the ancient ceiling and sent it splintering on the floor before me.

"Enough!" I shouted, and Belinda released her switch.

I leaped for Theo. His first response was to hurl the cross away from him. Mine was to grip the wrist that held the gun and slam it into the wall behind him.

The gun slipped from his grip, and I caught it, hurling it away into the chapel. I then pinned my forearm under his chin and thrust him back into the wall.

"Now, Theo," I growled. "Just you and me. Go for it!" I backed off a step or two, shouting to Belinda as I went. "Get out, girl. I want him alone!"

She hesitated a moment, then fled.

As the door slammed behind her, I noted the fire of excitement in Theo's eyes. He needed no coaxing. His hand slapped against his hip and came up with a stiletto every inch as lethal as Hugo.

I blinked.

Theo laughed. "She missed it in the search. Clever, isn't it? Taught to me by one of my finest pupils."

He gave a quick lunge, more for the purpose of testing reflexes than intent on any damage. I did my part. My hands took up a defensive stance, and my body backed off. Next came a feint, then a lunge.

"Good, Nick," he cackled, his face feverish with excitement. "Good form. Good stance. Learned your lessons well, I see."

I refused to take the bait. The man was pressing for the psychological edge, and I didn't go for it.

Quickly the knife flew into his left hand, a move designed to focus an enemy's attention on the blade, not the attacker. My eyes flew instead to his feet, studying the telltale signs of his shifting weight. The kick he let fly lacked the commitment of a sincere blow and was easily brushed off. He was still testing.

"Excellent!" he growled, his voice thick with condescension. "You've retained your master's status admirably."

"I'm tired of screwing around, Theo," I hissed. "Let's have at it, or I might get bored enough to just walk away from your little charade."

His look darkened. "Very well. It's time for the doctorals, N3. Are you good enough?"

"Let's find out, N1."

He steeled himself and lunged. The knife itself was easily parried aside.

Too easily.

At the same time, he twisted his body, launching his foot on a revolving kick to the head. This move too had its own counter, but the thought struck home that that counter would suddenly put me in easy reach of his knife hand.

Instead I raised my arm and took the brunt of the blow on my forearm, a blow that sent a numbing ache clawing up to my shoulder. I spun with the impact, content with the nicking bite of the blade as it slashed a tiny cut into my leg. Better the small wound to the thigh than the slashing one to the neck I would have received had I not changed direction.

And now it was my turn.

Theo had drawn his blood but opened himself up in the process. I continued the spin from his blow, then let fly a kick of my own. To his credit, Theo was in damn fine condition for a man who had occupied a desk for so long. He wasn't able to entirely avoid the blow, but he did manage to minimize it. I caught him in the chest and sent him reeling back a few paces.

He regained his balance, his breath gasping from the impact against his sternum.

"Yeah . . . you qualify, Nick. So now the final test, eh?"

The knife flew back into his right hand, and his eyes hooded over with concentration. When he came, it was in flurried thrusts—and in earnest. He was refusing to allow himself to get near enough for me to gain the offensive. I reacted to each attack, parrying with relative control and ease.

But still he would lunge, move me back, coax me

right, finesse me left . . . but never with the right thrust for a quick kill. I was just beginning to sense the reasoning behind his maneuvers, when their results gave him the advantage he sought.

He was guiding me toward the chapel's right, and it soon struck me as to why. The bone fragments from Theo's errant shot were littering the floor in that area. He could see them; I couldn't. I planted my foot and prepared to shift the course of our movement, but that was the second his planning paid off.

A small sliver of bone caught under my shoe, and the force of my momentum sent my leg flying out from under me. My balance had been calculated toward the attacker, and the slip was too sudden to allow me to reposition my body.

I arched back, then tumbled.

Theo wasted no time. The moment he saw me start to lean, he lunged. The knife twisted across his fingers like a deadly baton and settled neatly into his palm for an overhand thrust. I was barely able to catch his wrist as his weight settled and dropped over me. We crashed to the floor.

The knife dropped damn close to my throat, but I summoned my strength and managed to push it back up a few inches. Theo was grunting. His sweat dripped onto my cheeks as he struggled to bring the stiletto back down.

His left hand shot out and caught me under the chin, forcing my head back and opening up my throat for the final kill.

I tore at his wrist with my right hand, but most of my arm strength was lost from the blow I had taken earlier. Still I fought, twisting my body on the floor, trying in some way to shift the force of his pressure away from me.

It was during that twist that I felt it. A sharp prick of pain jabbed at my ribs. Were it not for the fact that I could see both of Theo's hands, I would have been convinced he had produced another knife. I rolled back, accepting the downward pressure of his thrust.

I kept my right hand clawing at his arm, knowing I couldn't remove that hand without Theo wondering why. I studied his face. He was intent on my throat, his eyes mad with the nearness of success.

I allowed the blade to gently start its fall. My right hand tore with even greater frenzy as the knife edged closer and closer to its target. With each descending centimeter, Theo's eyes grew wider and hungrier. He hardly felt it at all when my right hand slipped down to the floor.

There was only a second of groping before the object stabbed my wrist. My hand retreated, my fingers curling around a seven-inch length of fragmented bone. It was fractured to a razor's sharpness.

With a final twist of my head, I rammed the makeshift dagger home. I wedged it between Theo's ribs and twisted it, rooting for the man's heart.

There was an ear-splitting scream, and the stiletto dropped to the floor beside my face. An easy shove rolled him to the side.

I released my grip on the bone and looked over at Theo. His mouth gaped open, his eyes wide and glassy. He stared at me for a second, his lips curling into a smile.

"You win . . . I win," he said, and then death shook his body.

I got quickly to my feet. I stared down at him, disgust rushing through me. I then stared at the walls. There was a peaceful serenity to the faces that stared back.

As my eyes floated around the room, they caught

sight of Belinda. She was standing off in a corner of the sanctuary, Wilhelmina firmly in her grasp.

I looked at her and smiled.

"What the hell," she shrugged, moving to where I stood. "I just wanted to be sure."

"Yeah," I nodded. "Let's get the hell out of here."

Just outside the chapel, I made the call from an open booth. It would take a clean-up crew ten minutes to get there.

I hung up and grabbed Belinda's hand.

"What now?" she asked as I dragged her toward the piers.

"You suppose one of those boats over there can be hired?"

"I suppose so . . . why?"

"You ever looked up at the sky through a hole in the roof of a cave in the cliffs of the Algarve?"

"Can't remember that I have," she said, laughing.

"I mean, looked up from the bottom of a fisherman's boat gently bobbing in the water?"

"Sounds like a poor man's water bed."

I grinned and curled an arm around her waist.

"That's what I plan to make it."

# DON'T MISS THE NEXT NEW
# NICK CARTER SPY THRILLER

## *THE KALI DEATH CULT*

They followed, at least twenty armed men. As we walked, I became increasingly aware of others filtering down from the mountainside, like tiny droplets of water coalescing to form a torrential downpour. At the end of twenty minutes, I estimated a full one hundred men accompanied us. Yet their purpose wasn't clear; no one had said a word to us.

"How many men does the Old Man of the Mountains have?" I said to Dasai, my voice barely audible above the wind howling through distant crags.

"No one knows. Many. He commands totally in this part of the world. The British often fought him—unsuccessfully. They finally came to grips with the idea that he ruled and would not disturb them in the lower portions of the country. India has always been ruled by many, under the guise of one."

"You talk like the current leader is the one who lived a century and a half ago." To this Dasai said nothing.

"How much farther do we have to go?" I asked, after we'd been climbing a steep path for over an hour. No end was in sight as the stony ledge curved around a mountain.

"Who knows?" answered Ananda. "Few ever attempt to talk with the Old Man. We might be the first in a hundred years. Little information on these people gets out."

"But you said he controls most of northern Pakistan and India." I didn't understand what she meant.

"By fear. When your every waking moment is filled with dread and your dreams are haunted by monsters worse than reality, no one need stand over you. The Old Man of the Mountains inspires fear. His thugs control absolutely. The goddess is a bloody-handed one, too, demanding sacrifices often."

"Great, a cult devoted to killing. And we're in their territory." I unobtrusively touched the butt of Wilhelmina. She stayed in her holster. With eight rounds, I couldn't even put a dent in the men surrounding us. More than two hundred now stalked along behind us. It was as if the rocks themselves leaked humanity. More joined us as we continued up the impossibly steep, narrow pathway.

I chanced to look over the edge. At least a mile of empty space before solid ground. A touch of vertigo hit me. I wobbled and turned in to the mountain. The solid stone reassured me. I hoped the rocky ledge we walked over stayed put. I didn't like the idea of trying to sprout wings on the way down.

"Will we ever get to the top of this mountain?" I asked. "It goes on forever."

"We are nearing the Old Man's village," said Dasai. He pointed. I shook myself. It had to be oxygen starvation that I hadn't noticed earlier. The tricky stone path plastered to the side of the mountain had turned into a fitted block road. This kind of effort at this altitude wasn't made unless something important was nearby.

Every breath I took strained me to the utmost. The altitude robbed me of all but forty percent of the air I'd expect at sea level. If I hadn't been in good shape to start with, I'd be gasping like a fish out of water. As it was, I merely panted.

"We must enter," said Dasai, fear beginning to come into his voice.

"So?"

"The inscription on the gate reads 'Praise the Goddess Kali, Worship Her With Death To Unbelievers.' "

"Strong stuff," I said, then realized that meant me.

What the warning intended, I hoped, was to keep unbelievers out. The ones who weren't invited. Then I began to worry about our escort. Maybe they weren't inviting us in but rather showed us to the place of execution. We'd purposely invaded the Old Man of the Mountains' territory.

I shook off that idea. If he'd wanted us dead, there had been ample opportunity on the mountain. We'd have died and never known it. Still, from the history of Kali that Ananda had given me, the goddess was a vindictive bitch delighting in torture.

We walked through the gates. As they swung shut in a ponderous arc behind us, I felt as if I'd entered another world. Cut off, there was only one way to go—forward.

Almost a mile into the side of the mountain I had my next shock. We were on a rim overlooking the inside of the mountain. It had been hollowed out. A city bustled some thousand feet below, a complete city of at least a quarter million people. Distant torches flared and smoked, veiling the city in murk, but enough came through to impress the hell out of me. A complete civilization flourished at the top of the world, buried under an enormous mountain. I'd thought the gates and the stone pillars supporting them had been magnificent.

This hollowed out mountain and the city it contained ranked as the largest engineering project executed by man.

And it was totally unknown except to the followers of Kali living here.

"Down," came the curt command from a weathered man with bandoliers of ammunition crossing his thick chest. He carried an ancient rifle and when I didn't move, he pointed it. The road, a superhighway in width, snaked back and forth down to the floor where the city sprawled. I began walking, Dasai and Ananda following.

I had the distinct impression this mission had gotten out of hand, that even Nick Carter, Killmaster, was in over his head.

—From THE KALI DEATH CULT
A New Nick Carter Spy Thriller
From Charter in May

| | | |
|---|---|---|
| ☐ 33068-1 | **HIDE AND GO DIE** | $2.50 |
| ☐ 29782-X | **THE GOLDEN BULL** | $2.25 |
| ☐ 30272-6 | **THE GREEK SUMMIT** | $2.50 |
| ☐ 34909-9 | **THE HUMAN TIME BOMB** | $2.25 |
| ☐ 34999-4 | **THE HUNTER** | $2.50 |
| ☐ 35868-3 | **THE INCA DEATH SQUAD** | $2.50 |
| ☐ 35881-0 | **THE ISRAELI CONNECTION** | $2.50 |
| ☐ 47183-8 | **THE LAST SAMURAI** | $2.50 |
| ☐ 58866-2 | **NORWEGIAN TYPHOON** | $2.50 |
| ☐ 64433-3 | **THE OUTBACK GHOSTS** | $2.50 |

*Available at your local bookstore or return this form to:*

 **ACE CHARTER BOOKS**
P.O. Box 400, Kirkwood, N.Y. 13795

Please send me the titles checked above. I enclose _____.
Include 75¢ for postage and handling if one book is ordered; 50¢ per book for
two to five. If six or more are ordered, postage is free. California, Illinois, New
York and Tennessee residents please add sales tax.

NAME _____

ADDRESS _____

CITY_____ STATE ZIP_____

Allow six weeks for delivery.

A8